Tears
in the
Chambers
Of
Heaven

Trinisha Marks

DEDICATION

This book is dedicated to Faith Monet Love
your smile helped me to finish this book.
#mysecondminime

CONTENTS

You've kept track of my every toss and turn through the sleepless nights, Each tear entered in your ledger, each ache written in your book. (Psalm 56:8 MSG)

ACKNOWLEDGMENTS

I would like to thank God who gave me a story inside my soul to write

I would like to thank my husband Kevin, who held my hand until i could freely give him my heart my forever love. My six kids who are my heartbeat and send me into cardiac arrest at times.

My dad, Julian , mom Patricia and sisters and my "crazy brother" who was always encouraging me in my writing adventures... My favorite auntie you know who you are.

To Tammara my wonder twin you make my words make sense.
Tonya D. and Sharon P and my sisters Jessica and Dee who listened to my story lines over and over until it was perfected.

To Ladana and Sherricka who relentlessly went on a million errands and whatever else needed to be done I appreciate you both.

To Tammie Henderson who was the thorn in my side to push me in my final lap.

Ida Mae you are a phenomenal woman.

My friend who finished his course during the writing of this book Leonard Tatum I miss you so much but u are one of my favorite stories "everything and nothing".

Trina his forever love who story inspired me to not be bitter but better .

And to New Beginnings my "Family within Family" this is only the beginning! Pastor Bobby Smith and Elect Lady Smith I love you a "million tomorrow's "....thanks for your courage in the days of adversity.

this book is dedicated to my god daughter, Faith Love you inspire me to be better your smile helped me finish*

Prologue

The rays of sunshine began to creep into the room, threatening to dispel the dark shadows that lingered. Darkness clung to every corner it possibly could to keep from being overtaken. Proven not to be a worthy opponent for light, darkness fled quietly waiting for his next opportunity to strike.

Kathleen yawned, retreated underneath her oversized comforter, and took a deep breath. The smell of him lingered in the room even though he had been gone for nearly four months. Maybe it was because she could not bring herself to wash the sheets where he had lain or the fact that she still sprayed her pillow with his favorite cologne every night and slept in one of his oversized shirts just so that she could be next to him. She suspected that no amount of removing his things or his smell could ease her pain or propel her into a life without him.

She would not allow herself to take that long jog down memory lane, even though she did this every morning. As if she had given wretchedness her cue, sadness tugged at her heart. Kathleen submerged herself deeper beneath the comforter. How ironic, she thought, the very bed that had once held dreams, visions, late night talks and laughter now was just a bed, a bed that was filled with unwanted, yet savored memories.

She exhaled loudly as she uncovered herself and shrugged off the unwelcome caresses of the sunbeams. They were intruding into her world, and seemed to move carefully and delicately over her body as if to tease her, reminding her that she was still alive. This morning she did not want to be reminded that she was expected to live another day without him. She looked down at the small yet protruding ball that used to be her stomach. There was no doubt that she was pregnant. She wondered whether the baby would have Danny's piercing green eyes or her beautiful caramel skin and long curly multicolored hair that reflected reds and blonds, browns and blacks. Her mom had always referred to her hair as God's color palate.

She hadn't told a soul, not even Danny, because she found out two weeks after the funeral that she was pregnant. She had been a little tired and had missed her period. She thought it was stress. Kathleen made an appointment to see the doctor with the intention of getting him to prescribe her some sleeping pills because, no matter how hard she tried, she could not assuage her mind to sleep.

The doctor insisted on running additional tests to be sure it was just stress. When the doctor came in with what should have been the most wonderful news of any young woman's life, she just sat there and burst into tears. Bliss was the last thing she felt as she heard herself asking about her options.

The doctor quietly left the room. It seemed like forever as she listened to the beating of the clock as the minutes passed by. Then the doctor returned, thrusting into her hands two multi-colored pamphlets. One pamphlet was about abortion, and the other one was about adoption. She thought she would never in her life consider either option, but now when faced with the reality of being a single mom she couldn't rule out anything. Could she do it without Danny? Kathleen stared blankly at the doctor as he explained to her that right now the baby growing inside was just a bunch of dividing cells. She mumbled something inaudible as she stumbled out of the examination room, past the doctor and out into the lobby, which was filled with other women who were sharing birth stories and ultrasound photos as they cooed over fingers, toes and big heads. She wandered out of the office and into her car where she sat paralyzed for hours.

Kathleen picked herself up out of the bed and tried to focus as she dressed. It seemed like everything reminded her of him. She remembered their daily ritual dance. Kathleen would slip out of bed, careful not to wake him. Then she would brush her teeth, wash her face, spray a little perfume here and there and slip back into bed. Danny would stir shortly after she returned and he would slip out of bed, careful not to wake her, or so he thought. She laughed as she thought about how he would sit in his chair and watch her. Then orange and red colors would streak across the sky, beginning the duel between night and day as each struggled to have its way. He would kiss her and she would open her eyes. As they exchanged smiles, she would then reach her arms out to him, and they would escape to a place where only their love mattered. They would dance to a tune that only they heard.

Kathleen glanced in the mirror and wondered who this shell of a woman she hardly knew was. She saw the tears streaming from her eyes. Her mother had once told her that whenever God's children would cry, God would keep a record and the angels would come down, collect the tears, file them away, and store them in the chambers of Heaven. She wondered how many angels were there, collecting her tears to store away. One thing was certain; they were definitely working overtime. She cried a lot nowadays, probably because of hormones. Yet, deep inside she knew the pain came from a place where there was a hole she wasn't sure could ever be repaired. She used to pride herself with being confident when walking into a room and immediately commanding the attention of the room. People had always been captivated by her beauty, and when she talked, people always held onto her every word. These days she didn't even want to get out of bed. She seemed to dodge people, hoping she would avoid the stares and rambling questions like "How are you doing?" Did they really expect her to tell the truth? She feared her life would never be happy again, so she contemplated killing the only product left from her and Danny's love because she couldn't fathom somebody else raising "it" and didn't think she could do it herself.

Would she remember him every time she looked at their baby? Nobody wanted to hear how she was really doing. They wanted her to say, "Blessed and highly favored," words every good Christian was supposed to say. They wanted her to say that she somehow found the strength from God to carry on, that somewhere in the midnight hour, God had miraculously heard her cry and made everything alright! As she looked at the tear-streaked shell, she wondered if the old Kathleen had really existed at all, or was just a figment of a parallel universe, displaced briefly in a moment of time.

~

Oh, she knew God was real. Kathleen really had one question for Him. Did He hear her? The Creator who had the authority to part the Red Sea, could He get rid of the pain in her heart? Kathleen began to feel that familiar sickness as the sadness began to swell so deep in her heart that her very soul began to bleed. "Where are you God? I need you," she said. Kathleen waited in expectation of His reply, although she didn't know what she would say next had He given her the opportunity.

A cry began to permeate the room. She glanced around, expecting to see its originating point. The cry sounded so far away that she was surprised when she realized the cry was coming from deep within her. It sounded like a muffled moan. She was exhausted and her head ached. Her room sat still, eerily quiet offering no reply, no comfort, and no relief. She collapsed motionless, unable to utter another word.

She thought to herself, "I don't think I can do this today." She scurried like a little child back to her bed, fleeing from danger and retreating once again beneath her memories. However painful they were, these memories were her only connection to him.

The phone rang, jarring Kathleen back into reality. "Hello," she said with as much emotion as she could muster. "Hello," piped the cheery voice on the phone. It was Shirley, the president of the Sunshine Committee at her church, who just so happened to be her best friend. "Get up girl, we are going to breakfast." Before she could protest, Shirley hung up, leaving Kathleen holding the phone and listening to a dial tone blaring in her ear.

She could just call her back and come up with an excuse, but she knew Shirley would not take "no" for an answer. Rejection had never been one of her strong suits. It's funny that they had been friends since they were kids and Kathleen had never been able to say "no" to Shirley.

Kathleen had always been pretty popular, but when she had an occasional run in, Shirley had always been the one who had come to Kathleen's aide when things seemed to get too tough. Now, as fate would have it, the very person who had always made everything better, the person who knew just what to say to make everything better, didn't have the answers to make this better. Not even Shirley had the miracle she needed to protect her from the realization that Danny was really gone. She sighed heavily at the thought of trying to pick herself up out of bed. It seemed too over-whelming. She missed the little things that used to give her joy; now everything seemed pointless. She sighed with defeat and turned over with every intention of sleeping the day away. She would meet with Shirley, but just not today. Today, she would dream, and hope she would not have to remember. Yes, she would go to a place where he was still hers and she was still his. This was a place where the pain in her heart didn't exist, if for just a moment. She would embrace a life with him once more even if it were just a dream.

~

Shirley Hopkins

Shirley grimaced to herself as she thought of Kathleen. She knew that she was probably laying in her bed thinking about Danny. She wanted so much to offer words of encouragement, but she didn't know what to say. She laughed to herself. "Mrs. Sunshine," as the ladies of the church had affectionately named her, was speechless. She was always the one who would console the families after their loss; she always had the right words. Yet, when it came to her best friend, it was hard to know what to do or what to say any more since Danny's unexpected death. Her friend, who was once the life of the party, was now slowly dying right in front of her. She didn't know what to do to help her. Shirley had voiced her concern to Pastor Jameson after church on Sunday. His advice had been to give Kathleen her space; everyone grieves differently, and time would heal the pain. Shirley didn't think that he understood the seriousness of the situation. Then she thought to herself, "How could he? After all, no one knew Kathleen. Not like she knew her."

Shirley heard Brian's car pull up and she felt her heartbeat accelerate. She knew that every moment of life was precious, and she was reminded of that haunting fact whenever she thought about Kathleen and Danny. She knew that there had been a little distance between them lately. Brian had seemed very detached. It started after Danny's death. This morning would be different because she would concentrate on him. He was in for a surprise. She had fixed his favorite breakfast - sausage, eggs and homemade blueberry pancakes. She had even melted his butter and warmed up his syrup just as he liked it. She had bought a beautiful red chemise with a Japanese pattern, and it hung just right. She lit candles all around the living room. She had even dropped rose petals from their living room to the bathroom where she had drawn him a nice hot candlelight bath. Oh yea, she would make sure this was a morning he would never forget. She threw on a bathrobe and sprayed on his favorite perfume. She hurried to surprise him at the door. She laughed to herself. Yes, he was in over his head this morning.

Today, something was wrong. She could tell when he kissed her on the cheek instead of planting a kiss on her lips, which was his usual greeting. His face wore a solemn look. His mood was so somber. Then it came, the words no wife ever wants to hear: "Honey, I've been doing a lot of thinking about you and about me. I think that we have just grown apart." Brian then proceeded to inform her that after 15 years of marriage, he had fallen out of love with her and they needed a "break". He spoke about love as if it were a water faucet that flowed until it had fulfilled its purpose and could be turned off with a simple turn of a knob. She sat dumbfounded as he talked. It was almost as if her heart had stopped, and for a brief moment, she felt like she was going to get sick. His mouth continued to move slowly, expelling words that she could not understand. Then he stroked her arm almost as if he thought it would ease the blow. She felt a cold chill travel down her spine as she looked at him. Then he said, "I know all this shouldn't be a surprise; it's been coming for a while. We've been headed toward divorce for some months now. It was inevitable, Susie." Brian paused and looked at her as if expecting her to agree with him. Did he just say divorce? What about the "break"? Was he asking her for a divorce or was he just exploring possibilities? All this was happening much too fast. Susie! She couldn't believe that he had the nerve to call her the pet name he had given her years ago, in the same sentence as divorce!

His words rolled so easily off his tongue that Shirley was sure he had rehearsed this conversation over and over until he found just the "right" words. He rambled on nonchalantly without blinking. It was almost as if he had asked her what type of ice cream she wanted and now he was sitting there waiting for a response. Brian continued after a brief pause: "I think it's only fair that I let you stay in the house. I rented an apartment not too far from here. Besides, the house is important to you. What do you think?" After it took her so long to respond, he then said, "Or we could sell it?" Shirley swallowed the hard lump surfacing in her throat. It sounded like he had settled it in his mind. What did he want her to say, that she was okay with him moving out? Her mouth felt like it was filled with cotton as she struggled to bring forth the words to express how she felt. Her brain somehow could not process any of what he was saying. Almost as though in a daze, she heard herself ask him if he wanted coffee. He declined, of course. She turned around and left him standing right by the front door. It had been left open, and the morning air easily engulfed the heat that had once filled their beautiful home.

She busied herself looking for the coffee filters, only to find out that they had run out. She instead settled for tea and turned on the teakettle to boil her water.

"Do you want coffee?" That was the first thing that came to her mind. It sounded quite funny. She thought, "My husband tells me he needs a 'break' from our marriage, and all I have to say is, "Do you want coffee?" Her fingers trembled as she opened the dishwasher, looking for her favorite mug. She opened the tea bag, laid it in the mug, and then stared at the fire blazing under the kettle. What she really wanted to ask him was "How could he stand before her acting as if she was just some stranger he had just met?" She was the same woman who he had stood before fifteen years ago, with shaky palms and quivers in his voice as he vowed to love, honor and cherish her until death. "It's me!" she wanted to scream, the same woman to whom he pledged his undying love over and over in hushed whispers as they would lay entwined night after night in a lovers' embrace. She wanted to ask him why he felt like "they" weren't worth the fight.

How could he give up so easily? You don't just fall out of love overnight, or do you? She wanted to ask him if there was someone else, but she was too scared of what his response would be. She heard him close the door. She thought he had left. She listened for his key turning in the lock. When it never came, she turned around and saw Brian standing there looking at her. Neither one of them spoke. Her eyes searched his for just a glimmer that there was something still left, but instead she was greeted with a cold stare.

Her hands trembled uncontrollably, as she tried to keep her composure. She tried to take small sips of her tea, but it tasted bitter. She didn't have the energy to look for the honey, so she swallowed the tea. Shirley felt the mug slipping from her hands as she struggled to keep a grip, but her hands seemed to have lost their strength. Helplessly, she watched as her favorite mug went spiraling down toward the floor. It crashed to the floor and broke in many pieces with a loud earth-shattering clank. That sick feeling began to rise again, and this time she knew she was going to get sick. She turned and sprinted past Brian to the bathroom, leaving Brian alone once again. Shirley closed the door to the bathroom and stayed in there for what seemed like an eternity. She sat in their roman tub, balled up in a fetal position. It was the only place that seemed to offer her comfort.

Shirley heard the front door shut and hurried out of the bathroom as she heard Brian's car pull out the drive way. She looked out the window, just in time to see her life speed away. She turned around to see that he left his house key sitting on the island in their kitchen.

She got the broom and began to sweep up the pieces off the floor as she wondered who would be there to help her pick up the pieces of her life. Shirley finished and threw the shattered pieces in the garbage. She couldn't help but wonder, "Was her marriage like her favorite mug, escaping from her life forever?"

Shirley picked up the phone to call Kathleen, but when Kathleen answered, she could hear the depression and hopelessness in her voice. All Shirley could do was try to sound happy. She hurriedly asked her to breakfast and hung up the phone, partly because she knew that Kathleen would try to protest but also because she was scared. She was scared that if she said one more word to her, she would divulge everything. Kathleen was dealing with so much, she couldn't add to her burden. She vowed not to mention what was going on. Moreover, she rationalized the idea because, in truth, she didn't even know what was going on herself. Today, Shirley would focus on her best friend. Helping her would buy Shirley some time before she had to deal with her own messed up life.

~

Brian Hopkins

Brian's heart was beating so fast and loud that he swore Shirley could hear it as it began pulsating in his throat. He could hardly believe that she stood there so calmly when he felt like he was babbling, in search of words to tell the love of his life that he was leaving. Danny's death had thrown his life into a tailspin. Brian and Danny had spent so much time together, first because the girls would drag them along on their little escapades, then because they became friends - best friends. Danny really was the only one who knew everything about him, things he really couldn't tell Shirley because she would try to understand them, categorize and file them away. Some things could not be understood and filed neatly away. If anybody ever deserved a happily ever after, it was Kathleen and Danny. If they didn't get it, he felt like he and Shirley didn't stand a chance. If he were going to lose her, it would be on his terms. Then it wouldn't hurt as bad. He hurried out of the house and into his car because he knew that if she had just asked him to stay, then he would not have been able to leave. Brian had expected her to do something or say something to give him some kind of sign that maybe he was making the wrong choice; instead, she offered him coffee. He was confused. Did she want him to go? He had gone into the kitchen and had seen her making tea. He had thought then that she would ask him to stay. When she saw him come into the room, she threw down her mug -- her favorite mug -- and she ran out of the room. Did she really despise him so much that she didn't want to be in the same room with him? He wondered what was going through her mind.

She had been so busy with Kathleen lately; he hated himself for blaming her, but it was true. Shirley had seemed to lose interest in "them." They were growing more and more distant such that he had been looking for opportunities to stay out of the house. Brian began throwing himself into work. He figured it would pass, but days turned into months and somehow a wall had come in between them. Brian wasn't sure when it had happened.

Yet, one day he realized it was there, and he couldn't bear the thought of losing her. It had started before Danny's death, but in the last few months, the situation had gotten unbearable. If it weren't Kathleen, it would be somebody else. Shirley was always busy fixing somebody's life. He had met Shirley when he was 12 years old. The first time he saw her he had known she was the one. They had gotten married when he was nineteen. She had always been his sunshine, so he nicknamed her "Susie." It was kinda dumb, he thought. When he was a little kid, he had named the sun "Susie." When Shirley had come into his life, she was like his ray of sunshine after the storm of his parents' divorce.

She stepped in, helping him pick up the pieces after his dad moved out, leaving his mother a single parent struggling to provide for him and his sister by working two jobs. The day his dad left was etched in his memory forever. That was the last time he had seen or heard from him. Brian remembered stroking his sister's arm as she cried, trying to soothe her tears. He remembered all of it like it was yesterday. They both pressed their foreheads against the tear-streaked windowpane, begging their dad not to leave. Brian wasn't sure why his dad had left. As far as he knew, his mom and dad never had so much as an argument. Yet, as he watched his dad's car speed away down the narrow street, his mom stood as still as a statue, blinking as if trying to hold back the tears. She never spoke again of their father. It was almost as if the life they had shared together had never existed. He vowed that he would never forget his dad. Somehow, even as he struggled to hold on to the few memories he had over the years, he seemed to lose them. In fact, the only thing he remembered about his dad was the day he left.

He knew his "Susie" would be okay. She would go on her crusade of fixing lives although Brian wondered whether he would ever be the same. He somehow doubted that the ache in his heart would ever go away. He had lost Danny and if he was going to lose her, he needed to do it on his terms. He couldn't bear to have it any other way. He glanced in his rear view mirror and watched his home disappear from his sight. Brian pushed his foot harder on the accelerator. He needed to get away fast because he couldn't stand the actualization that his marriage was over.

Chamber one

Shirley sat outside Kathleen's house and wiped the tears from her eyes. She needed to pull herself together. She reached into her purse, pulled out her mirror compact and looked at her reflection. She applied a little makeup here and there. Although her appearance seemed to improve on the outside with a small stroke of a brush, she knew that she was going to need a lot of prayer to make it through the next couple of days. Shirley vowed to take things one day at a time, and right now, she needed to get Kathleen up and out of the house. She got out of her car, strolled up to the door, and knocked but there was no answer. She rang the doorbell. Still, there was no answer. Shirley fished for the key in the bottom of her purse. She knew that Kathleen was probably still in bed. Having retrieved the key, she turned the lock and opened the door. As the door swung open, she looked in horror at Kathleen's house.

The once immaculate house was littered with trash and had a repugnant smell. She hurried toward the kitchen to see that old Chinese food was the culprit of the foul odor. Shirley picked up her cell phone and dialed her housekeeper. Maria promised to stop by and clean up Kathleen's house today. Shirley told her that she would leave the key under the flowerpot and thanked her. She then proceeded up the winding stairs toward Kathleen's bedroom. Shirley started down the long hallway when two multicolored leaflets, sitting on the computer desk in Kathleen's loft area, caught her eye. Shirley gasped when she read what the contents were about. Did this mean that?

No, certainly Kathleen couldn't be! But why else would she have these? She noticed a white paper tucked into the pamphlet revealing Kathleen's positive test results. Kathleen was pregnant. "Oh, my God!" she said out loud and glanced around the seemingly abandoned house for more clues. Certainly, she wasn't really contemplating an abortion, or worse, had she already gotten an abortion? Did she not know the precious gift that she had growing inside? Adoption? Would Kathleen really give her baby to someone else to raise?" Many questions raced through Shirley's head. How far along was she? It had to be Danny's baby, but why hadn't she told her? They were best friends, closer than sisters. What other secrets about Kathleen did she not know? And what should she do now that she knew?

She sat down at the desk, suddenly feeling overwhelmed. Was she too late? Shirley began to pray, "Oh God, give me the words to say. I am in over my head. I need you to speak a word into my spirit, a word that Kathleen needs to hear. God, please tell me I am not too late!" Just for a moment, Shirley remembered how happy she had been when she found out that she and Brian had been expecting a baby. When they had found out it was a girl, they were elated. She and Brian had decorated the nursery with beautiful pastel colors, put the crib up and placed clothes in the closet in preparation for the long awaited arrival of their bundle of joy. But when Shirley was twenty-one weeks pregnant, she left work early, complaining of cramps. She thought they were contractions but wasn't sure. When she called Brian, he insisted that she go to the hospital, telling her that he would meet her there.

The nurse led her to this little room, and they hooked her up to the monitor that was supposed to measure the contractions. The nurse said everything was fine. Then the doctor came in, took a single glance at her and released her. He ordered her to drink more water because she was a little dehydrated.

Shirley's eyes began to fill with tears as she remembered being at home and still in pain. Since she had never been pregnant before, she thought maybe she was having Braxton Hicks contractions. Shirley would often have bad bouts of vomiting. The doctors said it should pass, but she was sick most of the time. She would just concentrate on the baby growing inside her, that all of this was temporary.

This particular morning when Shirley sat up in her bed, her stomach felt queasy. She asked Brian to get the garbage can out of the bathroom. She began to vomit, but this time she felt something strange. It felt like something fell in her stomach, which was the only way she could describe it. Shirley hurried into the bathroom and sat on the toilet. She felt something that had a plastic like feeling between her legs. She could still hear herself screaming as she called Brian, and she remembered the look on his face as he called the doctor's office.

They rushed her into the emergency room and placed her in an examination room with five other women, separated only by curtains. She could still remember the cold chill as her teeth chattered partly from the cold air circulating through the room and partly because Shirley knew, something was not right. She felt panic rise up in her chest and she began to pray, "Lord, please save my baby!" She felt peace because she just knew that God was going to save her baby girl, despite the nurse's panic as she checked her to see how far along she was dilated.

The nurse dashed out of the room. Then Shirley was surrounded by technicians poking and prodding her. The cold goop slid down her belly as they performed an ultrasound. She looked at the small screen that showed images of her baby. Everyone left the room to have some kind of conference.

Brian came in and the look on his face said everything she did not want to know. He grabbed her hand. Then another doctor came into the room introducing himself as a high-risk doctor. He had a name she could not even pronounce. He told her that she suffered from a condition that was very rare in her age group. She was only twenty years old at the time. He then proceeded to tell her that she had an incompetent cervix that was incapable of holding a pregnancy through full term. He also informed her that she was already dilated to six and fully effaced. He told her that there was no possibility that her daughter would live if she gave birth now; the baby just wasn't developed enough.

He informed her that nothing could be done to stop "it" from coming. He reassured her that she would be able to have other kids in the future. He was so cold and impersonal. Shirley was having a hard time comprehending that this baby, her baby that she felt kicking and turning somersaults would not be alive in just a few short hours.

She pressed her hand on her stomach, and it was almost like she felt her baby girl press her hand against hers as if to say, "Mommy, don't worry." Shirley said another prayer, "Please Lord, please save my baby." Her heart was filled with confidence once more that God had heard her plea and that He was going to save her baby. She did not care what the doctor said. He was not God. Her mind raced as she picked up the phone and called Kathleen to come and pray. She needed someone to touch and agree with her that her baby would live and not die.

The doctor focused his attention on Brian and asked him if he had any concerns. They sat there talking about her like she was not in the room. They were talking about the chances of it happening in another pregnancy. How dare they talk about her baby like she was already gone? Everything was going to be okay. God had always answered her prayers, and she just knew that if anybody was going to get a miracle, it was going to be her. She heard the doctor say that there was a ten percent chance that she would not go into labor and maybe hold the fetus another couple of weeks until it was visible.

Her baby was not an "it," and certainly, the doctor didn't know that when you have Jesus, you don't need percentages on your side. God was going to work and do what He as a doctor could not. The hours passed and Kathleen had come. They prayed. She stayed by her side until Shirley had asked her to leave and stop fussing over her. She was so sure she would be okay. God was going to answer her prayer. Shirley could still remember listening to the heartbeats of the other ladies' monitors in the room. It was almost as if the babies' heartbeats were playing some sort of cadence, sounding like horses galloping off to war.

One woman was pregnant for the eighth time, and all of them had different daddies. She was cussing her boyfriend out; he said he wasn't coming to the hospital because he was shooting hoops with his boys. Shirley wanted to scream when the lady then proceeded to complain about everything. There was another young girl who must have been about fourteen, and she was having twins. She was curled up in the bed with her teddy bear. She looked so tiny with her huge protruding stomach that resembled a beach ball. She felt very bad for the little girl as she lay alone crying. She wondered where this girl's mother was. Here she was a baby herself about to be propelled into womanhood.

Her OB doctor came into the room. Dr. Edwards was the sweetest man you could ever meet. He reminded her of a cartoon character. Hope filled her heart as she saw him. Shirley just knew that he was going to tell her everything was okay. But her heart dropped when she saw the tears fill his eyes as he struggled to find words to console her. She felt fear grip her heart again as she realized for the first time the seriousness of the situation.

It was a little bit after 9:00 pm when a private room opened up and Shirley was wheeled into a small room. Her stomach began to get that familiar feeling, as she struggled not get sick. She held it for as long as she could, and then she had to let it go. Her body wrenched side to side as she began to dry heave; then she heard a loud pop. Her water had just popped. The contractions began to hit her body immediately. Her room was filled with doctors, and she heard the high-risk doctor telling her to push. She didn't want to push. Each push was leading her daughter closer and closer to death.

Shirley pushed between prayers. She knew this baby was going to be born, so she prayed for her daughter. "Lord, please help her! God, save my baby!" Then at 9:23 p.m., she gave birth to a baby girl. She named her Destiny because she was destined to be born. Destiny lived for a few short hours and then took her last breath. The doctors continued to tell her how beautiful her baby was and how perfect she was. They tried to console her by telling her she would have another baby but Shirley wondered, "Did they not know that a million kids would never ease the pain of losing one?" Shirley wondered how you could love someone so much that you had just met and how could you miss someone so much you never really knew.

Shirley and Brian had to bury their daughter. She never would forget lying in the bed with her back to Brian and hearing him sobbing on the phone as he told his mom the baby had just died. He sobbed so hard; it was the first time she had seen Brian really show any emotion. Her heart broke. She was his wife. She was supposed to make it better. She couldn't. She didn't even know what she was supposed to feel.

From that time on, she had a hard time really showing any real emotion. After that, she couldn't cry, almost as if there was a wall that prevented her from experiencing anything good or bad. The memory of seeing Brian walk down to the gravesite with the little white box that held their daughter still haunted her until this day. Shirley had never really gotten over the death of their daughter. Shirley had read later that the problem she had was quite common in women between twenty through twenty-five weeks of pregnancy and could only be diagnosed by performing an ultrasound. She had blamed herself for so long. If only she had just insisted on an ultrasound, Destiny would still be alive today. She wondered that if she loved her daughter so much, why she could not bear to go to the gravesite where she was buried.

Shirley would often have dreams of Destiny, and it all started out the same. She would hear a baby crying, and she would look for her. Then the dream would shift to a log cabin and at first, her baby would be lying motionless on the couch. As she would get closer, she would see the baby beginning to move and her heart would fill with so much joy as she would hold her little baby. Once awake, she would cry for hours. There was nothing she could do for Destiny now. But Shirley was on a divine mission to save Kathleen from making a decision that she would regret for the rest of her life.

~

Kathleen slipped in and out of sleep. She thought she heard the door open, but she knew it was only Shirley. She struggled to sit up as she waited for her to come bouncing in. When she didn't after a few minutes, she pulled the comforter over her head, took a deep breath, and dozed back off to sleep. A little while later, she was awakened by Shirley opening the blinds and bouncing on the bed. "Get up!" she said, "Let's go get something to eat." "I'm not hungry," Kathleen murmured. She put the pillow over her head. Then it dawned on her. How was she going to get up and pass Shirley without Shirley noticing her belly? She had been successful in wearing baggy clothes that hid her small soccer ball of a belly. She went from dressing in sexy skintight clothes that accentuated her assets to big oversized clothes. She doubted that anyone even gave it a second thought especially since the majority of her days were spent by herself these days. "Give me some privacy," Kathleen said to Shirley, hoping that she would leave the room and let her get up to get ready. "Whatever Kathleen," Shirley said. "You don't have anything I don't have myself. Or do you?" she said jokingly. Kathleen sighed heavily and tried to wrap the comforter around her as she got out of the bed. She went into her bathroom and took herself a nice hot shower. The water felt good as it rolled across her muscles, soothing every inch of her body.

Kathleen had to admit just getting up and taking a shower made her feel better. She tried on a pair of jeans that used to be loose but now felt snug. Kathleen realized she needed to buy some more clothes. She couldn't help but glance at her stomach. She tried to remind herself that it was just dividing cells. Deep inside, she knew she could not let herself be attached until she was sure what she was going to do. She didn't have time to think about this now. It was going to take all of her strength to make it through the day. She glanced at herself once more, hurriedly applied her lipstick and then returned to her room where Shirley had made herself comfortable. She was lying down on her bed, looking at a magazine. Even though Shirley looked calm, something seemed different. She was trying too hard to be her normal self. Kathleen was bewildered. What could it be? Then she took a good look at Shirley, and she knew exactly what that look meant. It was all too familiar. Yep, she knew that look all too well. There was a dim light in her eyes where once there had been fireworks. It had to be only one thing. Brian.

Shirley was so uneasy, she didn't know what to say and how to say it. What if she was too late? Maybe she wasn't. Kathleen had grabbed the blanket to keep from exposing herself when she had gotten out of bed. Kathleen had never been that private, not in front of her. Then Shirley began to think that everything seemed to fit, the big clothes and all the time she spent by herself. Why wouldn't she have said something to her? Why was she choosing to go through all of this by herself? Kathleen had to know that she was there for her but how could she help her if she insisted on keeping her out of her life?

Yes, Shirley was hiding a secret too, but nothing like Kathleen. And who could blame her? She was justified in keeping her secret. Shirley was protecting her friend. Her anger turned to amusement as she thought to what lengths Kathleen had gone to hide her pregnancy.

Brian opened the door to his apartment and looked in disgust. One thing was certain - this was not home. The bare walls and lack of furniture reminded him of every time he came home. He would have to do something to decorate a little bit if he were going to stay here. He knew just the person for the job, a friend of his named Gwendolyn. She had an eye for color, and he just needed to make this place livable. He picked up the phone to call her and just for a moment, he paused. It was as if something told him not to call her, but just as it came, it went. He continued dialing. He really didn't expect her to answer anyway. He would just leave her a message, but she did answer and she seemed a little surprised when he told her the nature of his call.

Gwendolyn said she was in the area and would be right over. Brian went to the fridge and looked in. He had forgotten to get groceries. Then he remembered Shirley's food. Shirley could cook the most ordinary thing and make it taste extravagant. His mouth watered as he thought about her pot roast and potatoes. She had a way of seasoning meat just right; the girl knew she had it going on. She would sit at the table and just enjoy watching him savor every bite, and savor he did. Man, he missed that girl already and not just for her cooking. Well, he would have to get used to a bachelor's life. It was safer this way - no ties, just the way he wanted. Yet, he couldn't help but think about the softness of her skin and the little mole on the back of her neck. How good she would smell! Man, that girl was intoxicating! Before he could get lost in his thoughts all over again, the doorbell rang. He was glad for the distraction, but as he opened the door he couldn't help but notice the small ball of dread beginning to form in the bottom of his stomach.

Breakfast went without a glitch. Kathleen was glad, although there were plenty of uncomfortable pauses. Shirley definitely did not want to talk about Brian, which confirmed Kathleen's suspicion that something was going on. When she had tried to press the issue, Shirley had clamped down all together. Kathleen thought a couple of times she saw an accusing look in Shirley's eyes, but she wasn't sure. Well, anyway, it was good to get out of the house. Though she would never admit that to Shirley, she hated when she was right. She was happy to be spending time with Shirley, and why shouldn't they have fun? Almost like old times except they both had the cares of the world on their once carefree shoulders.

Shirley felt like the charade had gone on long enough. She casually asked her, "So, what's really going on?" She paused, giving her plenty of time to respond. When Kathleen started talking about going back to work, she held her cool for as long as she could. Then she said, "So heifer, when were you going to tell me?" Kathleen tried to look shocked and asked her what she talking about. Shirley wasn't in the mood to play games. She knew her secret, and she wanted details.

Kathleen felt the blood rushing to her face. Oh no, could she mean? No she couldn't possibly know, could she? She thought maybe she would test the water with small talk; but from Shirley's expression, she already knew. "Yes I am pregnant," said Kathleen. Just saying those words to Shirley was liberating. It wasn't as if she was by herself anymore. When Shirley had asked her why she had waited so long, she took a moment to collect her thoughts. Why had she waited so long? Was it because she had hoped to have made her decision by now? Kathleen began to cry. She was happy her friend knew, but what would she think if she knew she had already made the appointment for the consultation about having the abortion. Would she think she was a horrible person? Could Shirley be neutral despite her own experience with her daughter's death? This appointment was just a consultation visit. She changed her mind every second, yet at this moment she felt like an abortion was her final decision. She felt her heart sink when Shirley said she would not support her decision to have the abortion. See, that's why she had waited so long. If she had just been able to hide it a little while longer, it would have all been over with. Kathleen's eyes were so swollen from crying that her face hurt. Shirley told her there was no way that she would be a party to murder. Her liberation was short lived when Shirley looked her dead in her eyes and told her to pray and ask God to replace her fear with joy. Then she said that if God didn't think she was capable of raising this baby, she would not have been given the task.

Kathleen's frustration turned to anger as she glared and informed Shirley that her so- called God wasn't interested in talking to her. It was the truth. She never felt farther from God than she did right now at this very moment. Things only got worse from then on, and Shirley told her to grow up and stop feeling sorry for herself. Danny was gone, but this was how he would live on.

The words stung, and Kathleen stared at her friend's cold expression and gathered up enough strength to storm out of Shirley's car up to her house. When she opened the door, to her annoyance the house was clean. Although Kathleen knew it was juvenile to be upset and that Shirley only wanted the best for her, right now she wanted her stinky house back and for everything to be like it was. She wanted to just close her eyes and remember what the world used to be like before she was rudely jolted into a cold world. With her innocence of happy endings long gone, she was now alone, and she had no clue as to what to do get her life back. She was slowly dying, and the worst part was she wasn't sure she wanted to live.

Shirley was so mad; she wanted to be supportive, but somebody needed to say something. Kathleen could not just waste away because Danny was gone. She tried to be quiet, but she could not sit there and listen to her complain when God had blessed her with a baby. Shirley began to pray right there in the driveway of Kathleen's house. "Lord, please help my friend. I know You have given her this baby for a reason, and I'm asking you to intervene somehow, Lord. She is hurting, and I don't know what to do. I don't know how to make this better. Give me the words. Lord, please save this baby." Once she said the words, the pain of the loss of her own daughter hit the pit of her stomach. She doubled over in pain and let out a loud scream. "Lord, please save this baby," she cried over and over again. "Lord, please," she cried as she was reminded of the pain of losing her baby. Why after so many years, did she still feel like she would fall apart at the mention of her daughter's name?

Gwendolyn stood at the door, smoothed her skirt and tried to think why Brian was decorating an apartment. Did this mean that he had moved on from Shirley? A handsome man like himself deserved better, if he had in fact moved on. He would probably have certain "needs" by now, so she would have to make herself available. After all, he called her. It wasn't like she called him. She knocked on the door, and the door swung open. Man, he was finer than she remembered. He had that dreamy look in his eyes. He was wearing a crème cashmere sweater with chocolate colored slacks. She had always thought that his cocoa colored skin was beautiful. She could get lost in his hazel eyes. Man, God knew what He was doing when He created man, stood back, and said, "It is good", and Brian sure was good. Oh boy, she thought as she walked in past him and got a whiff of the best smelling cologne she had ever smelled. It made her heart skip a beat. She could just see herself getting lost and traveling through love's rolling waves of passion.
He was cool and collected as he offered her a drink and, of course, she declined. She was here "strictly for business." She would be back for pleasure, but right now this was just business.

Gwendolyn had met Brian when she had decorated his

office when he had made partner at a pretty prestigious law firm. Most people would have given their right arm for his job, so she was surprised when a few years later she had heard from a mutual friend that he had resigned and went to work as a freelance photographer. She had heard that he went from making a six-figure income to barely making ends meet. Maybe Shirley had gotten tired of picking up the slack. She smiled to herself. She knew how to appreciate a man with ambition, especially if he was as fine as Brian was.

Brian was pleasantly surprised at Gwendolyn's ideas for the house. She had decided to paint the walls, add some leather furniture, and a few plants; plus, she asked to use some of his photos to finish the look.

To tell the truth, her ideas were interesting, especially her choice of colors. It was just nice to have some company. She had asked him about Shirley, but he didn't answer her. He changed the subject, and she reluctantly moved on. It was late when she had finally left. She promised to make him a top priority in the coming weeks and "to make his house a paradise". Brian knew the decorations would help his house look better, but all the decorations in the world could not make it a home. He put the sheets on the futon, the only piece of furniture he had. He tried to sleep, but thoughts of Shirley plagued him, and he found himself once more longing to go home.

Shirley stared at the water in her glass. She would really much rather have had coffee, but she had promised to take better care of herself. After all, if she didn't, who else would? She had begun taking water aerobics at the fitness club, and she was feeling great for the first time in years. She missed Brian. She had seen him a couple of times since he moved out. Maybe there was still something left to be said since he had not officially filed for divorce nor said anything else about the house. He looked well, but she could tell that he missed her.

One indicator was the fact that he drove over to the house one time because he had said he needed to get a toothbrush. Yeah, right. He came by to see her. The drug store was closer than her house. Shirley had stopped by to drop off his mail a couple of days ago. She had to admit his pad looked pretty nice, but she had heard through an acquaintance that Gwendolyn had been hanging around his house. She had known the very first time she had seen her that she was no good. When she had told Brian, he had just laughed and told her not to worry. Sometimes Brian was so naïve. This was just one of those times that the woman in her knew when there was danger prowling. Although she was the best interior decorator one could find Gwendolyn's judgment had not been too good. She always seemed to get tangled up with married men. Her last rendezvous had almost gotten her killed. That woman was crazy. The wife had tried to run her over when she had seen her with her husband. Gwendolyn was not the problem in their case. Shirley was beautiful and confident, and she knew Brian.

Yes, he had kinda thrown her a curve ball when he moved out. One thing was for certain though, he loved her, and she loved him. Most importantly, she knew that her husband knew God. She was sure that God had brought them together and nobody was going to separate them. Shirley had also been sure to leave him something to remember her by. When she took him his mail, she planted a passionate kiss on his lips and let her perfume awaken his senses as she held him pressing her body against his in a long embrace. Some of it was for him, but some of it was to mark what belonged to her. Just because she was a Christian didn't mean that she didn't know how to "put it down". And she wanted him to remember that! If he wanted to play the game, she knew how to play it. And play well, she had to add. Shirley kept her conversation limited and answered pretty much only yes or no questions. She had to admit it was harder and harder every time she saw him to let him go. The last time she had seen him, she almost asked him to come home. Then she thought about it. She missed him, but she needed it to be his decision to come home because it was his decision to leave. If he was going to come back, he was going to have to be committed to her. She wanted all or nothing. She missed Brian, but most of all she missed her girl. It had been a few weeks since her spat with Kathleen. Things between them had been funky, but she was her girl, like it or not. Kathleen's appointment was today. She had gone for her consultation visit alone, and she seemed to be sure this is what she wanted to do. Shirley gave up on convincing her to have the baby. She had asked her to have an ultrasound anyway. If Kathleen could just see the baby, it would make her admit this baby was alive, not just a bunch of dividing cells, which was nothing but a lie from the pit of hell. Shirley remembered how deeply it had affected her to see her baby on the screen for the first time. Kathleen had just about chewed her head off, saying she just wanted it to be over with. Shirley knew that the circumstances did not outweigh God's purpose for this child. She had just finished reading The Purpose Driven Life, and something radical had taken place. She had peace, and for the first time she knew God had a purpose for her. She wasn't really sure what, but just knowing that she was not an accident gave her that peace.

All these years she had allowed the Devil to tell her she was worthless, rejected and unlovable. She knew that God loved her, and He had called her by name from the foundation of the earth. God loved her! He really loved her!

Shirley's mom Catherine had been raped while walking home from work. Shirley was the product of that rape. Her mother had kept her only because she didn't have the money for an abortion. Her mother's husband Mitchell had said that he would raise her as his own. He was a Christian man, and he did not want Mama to get rid of her. Daddy had been true to his word, never making any differences.

In fact, everyone had accused him of loving her more. They had a special bond. She would sit at his feet for hours, listening to him tell stories. He had a beautiful laugh, and he loved to laugh. They would just laugh at the silliest things. Daddy was a big man; he was 6'4 and weighed 400 pounds. Most people thought Daddy was intimidating, but when it came to Shirley, Daddy was so gentle. He loved to pray, and she could still hear Daddy's voice as he would walk the squeaky floor declaring the word of the Lord over his family. He had always said that the prayer mantle would someday be passed on to Shirley, and she was going to bring healing to many people. Daddy loved her. Somehow, she thought that his love might have been the source of her problem. Everyone was jealous. Her mother never let her forget that she was a product of something other than love. In fact, it was almost as if her mother had decided that she was going to give birth to her, but she was not going to love her, so she grew up in the house with her Mama but really without a Mama. Truth be told, she was sure she never did love her because she looked at Shirley with disgust. She remembered as a little girl her sister had been on a bike and ran into her standing right there on the sidewalk. Her sister had a small bruise; she and Camille both cried out for Mama, and her mother walked right past her to Camille. She scooped her up and kissed her and together they walked into the house, leaving Shirley alone bleeding and crying. It had been Daddy who had come to her rescue when he had pulled in from work and seen her laying there on the sidewalk. He picked her up, dusted her off and dressed her wound. Later on that night, she lay listening to Mama and Daddy arguing, and her Mama had admitted to him that she wasn't capable of loving such a child.

Her Mama and Daddy had two other children. The oldest was Camille. She was the star of the family, traveling all over the world modeling for some of the nation's top designers. Camille was twelve and Shirley was ten when Alex came along. Alex was the surprise Mama had, though she was going through the change of life. Surprise! Eight months later, here he came. He was her boy wonder who could never do anything wrong. Of course he would never grow up either because Mam would never let him. She still did everything for him because she swore that he was delicate since he had been diagnosed with a heart murmur when he was three months old. It didn't matter that he was twenty-four years old and still didn't have a job. You would think that Camille and Shirley would have been closer, considering that Camille was two years older than Shirley, but somehow she had always resented Shirley. Yet things were still tolerable. When Daddy died, things got real bad. They didn't even want her to come to the funeral. The last time she had talked to them was at the gravesite where they stood huddled together and glared angrily at her like she had killed him. Mostly Camille, in her big movie star glasses with body guards surrounding her. Shirley thought they had gone way too far when the bodyguards had insisted on running a metal detector across anyone who wanted to get close to Camille.

Alex, of course, fainted at the gravesite, complaining of his heart. Just for a moment Shirley thought she had seen what may have been remorse in her mother's eyes. Maybe even love, but it was soon replaced with hatred and contempt just as quick as it had come. Shirley had every intention to make things right with them if possible, especially with her mother. She was a product of her mother and couldn't really hate her own flesh and blood, could she? It would take a lot of prayer before she would embark upon that journey.

Of course the first thing she had wanted to do was to call Kathleen and share her newfound freedom. Even though Kathleen didn't want to hear about God, she was glad that Shirley seemed to have found some peace in her life. One thing that Shirley knew was that God was going to do something marvelous today. She had been praying and fasting, and she was sure God was going to do something. She didn't know what, but that was His problem to figure out. All she needed was faith.

Kathleen sat on the edge of her bed and thought, today is the day all of this will be behind her and she could move on. Kathleen wished Shirley would change her mind. She really could use the support. After all, she was her best friend, but Shirley could be quite stubborn. Kathleen was surprised her friend was going on and on about this new book she had read. It was apparent Shirley was excited, but when she heard her say she was going to talk to those crazy people she called family, Kathleen couldn't help but secretly pray that they would not reject her yet again like they had done in the past. Although Shirley seemed confident in her newfound purpose, she couldn't help but feel protective. These people were vicious and had not caused her friend anything but pain. She picked up the phone and thought about dialing Shirley, but she didn't have the energy to fight with her, so she placed the phone down on the cradle and began to get ready for the day that was going to change her life.

Brian sat across from Gwendolyn and was waiting for her to give him the figures for the newly decorated apartment. She had been very vague when he had asked her the price and insisted on him having dinner with her to go over the invoices. He was tired, having spent most of the day dealing with a new client who thought that the world should cater to her. Either she was going to hire him or not, but he was not about to jump through hoops to please her. It was a pretty healthy amount of change and he really could use it, but he had to draw the line somewhere. He knew he was talented and once everyone realized that too, then landing big accounts would be a piece of cake. One thing he had liked about Shirley was she was always his biggest fan, even when he had quit the law firm to take pictures. As his family would say, she had supported him and adapted. He was making good money at the firm, and it had been a struggle at first, but Brian had done well, and although work sometimes was a little slow, he was clawing his way to the top. Shirley. That girl was something else. She had surprised him when she had dropped by his house. She had brought him his mail and left him speechless when she kissed him. Even after she had left, he had smelled her perfume. He could not get her out of his head. Gwendolyn interrupted his thoughts as she asked him why he was sitting across from a beautiful woman and was daydreaming.

"Look, Gwendolyn, just tell me how much I owe you and we can call it a night. I'm kinda tired," he said. He saw what he thought was a spark in her eye, but he was tired of playing games. He was not the least bit amused.

Gwendolyn sat, planning her next maneuver. She wanted him, and was certain that she would make her move tonight. He seemed a little agitated, so she needed to be a listening shoulder. Get inside his head and see what he was thinking. She swirled around the glass of ice that had held Coke a few minutes ago as she sat there staring at him.

He was everything she ever wanted in a man. Brian was the first person who had given her the time of day when she had first moved to town. After her last boyfriend's wife tried to kill her, she moved to Vegas, hoping for a fresh start. Gwendolyn had met Brian and found out quickly he was not like any of the other men she knew. She was drawn to him. She didn't know why. Yes, he was good looking, but there was something else. She couldn't quite put her finger on it.

Brian definitely wasn't like the other guys who were only after her body. Once they had acted out their little fantasies -- you know the ones that their wives would not perform -- they would quickly discard her and go back to their wives. And she would be left with a sack full of dreams that would never be fulfilled. In truth, she wanted someone to look at her the way Brian had looked at Shirley. She wanted someone to live out her fantasies with. She knew he would never get involved with her as long as he was with his wife, but now was her opportunity. They were, after all, separated, and she was planning to walk through the open door, since it had presented itself.

You know what they say, one woman's junk can be treasured by somebody else. Now that Shirley had put him out, he was free game, and Gwendolyn was more than happy to take his mind off of Shirley. Maybe, just maybe, he might actually fall in love with her.

Kathleen entered the clinic and began filling out the paper work. All this was supposed to be done. She had filled out the paper work at the consultation. Yet, now this nurse was telling her she had to do it all over again. These people were incompetent. If they could not keep up with paper work, could she trust them with her life?

She hurried through the information and handed it to the nurse, who looked at her in disgust.

Kathleen was sure this woman probably thought she had her figured out. Whatever, she was sure of one thing, this woman could not possibly imagine all that she had been through in a few short months. She just wanted all this to be over with. She felt what she thought was a gas bubble raising inside her stomach. It's probably nerves, she thought to herself as she took her seat next to a middle-aged woman. She couldn't help but wonder what her story was. She didn't have to wait long. This woman started talking, and Kathleen began to regret her choice in seats as the woman told her of the affair she had engaged in. Her name was Marie, and she was a firecracker. She told her the long drawn-out version of her twisted affair. Kathleen glanced around, scanning for empty chairs when she heard Shirley's voice. She felt so relieved. Deep down inside, Kathleen knew that Shirley would not let her go by herself. She saw the worried look on Shirley's face as she came toward her.

Her friend embraced her, and suddenly it was like old times. She laid her head against her shoulder and cried. She knew everyone's attention was on her, but she didn't care. Kathleen felt like she was a little kid who was scared to death as she clung on to Shirley. It was almost as if she knew everything was going to be okay. Time stood still for one moment as these two friends fought to hang on to the present, afraid of what the next second would bring.

"Kathleen," called the nurse, as the door swung open. That gas bubble began to rise again in her stomach. It almost felt like little butterflies trapped in her stomach and deciding it was a good time for them to dance the waltz. She stumbled toward the door. Shirley tightened her grasp on her hand almost as if to assure her that she was not going to let her go. They walked together toward the door. The nurse said, "Which one of you guys is Kathleen because that's the only one I'm allowed to let come back here?" Kathleen haggled with the poor nurse so much that she promised to let Shirley come back after the initial exam, but before they began the procedure. She mumbled something about not getting paid enough to deal with people like Shirley. She said it wasn't company policy, but she would let it slip this time. And then she led Kathleen through the hallway of the clinic. She felt like a sheep being led to slaughter. Kathleen felt like her feet were laid in concrete. She was suddenly aware of how heavy her legs were. She struggled to take step after step. It was almost as if she had forgotten how to walk, and the gas bubble would not subside. It kept floating from side to side. The nurse led her to a room in the very back of the clinic. It was so small she felt claustrophobic as the walls slowly began to close in on her.

The nurse handed her a gown and a cup and told her to leave a urine sample in the bathroom. She left the cup in the cabinet in the bathroom and headed to her room. She wanted to run, but she prayed, "Lord, if You hear me, You need to answer me in some way that I know what I need to do!"

It was cold in the waiting room. Shirley looked around at the other girls there and wondered what their stories were. Some of them looked so young. They looked way too young to be having sex. "Man, girls start younger and younger". she thought as her attention focused on this beautiful redhead. She was a young girl named Nicole, and as they talked, she found out that this girl was only seventeen and her boyfriend had told her to get rid of the baby. This was her consultation visit. She looked afraid and eager to have some friendly company. Shirley instantly took a liking to this girl. Nicole was such a free spirit, but this boy she was wrapped up in was nothing but trouble. He was twenty-three and a college student.

Shirley had given Nicole her number in case she wanted to talk. She wanted to say much more, but she didn't want the girl to think she was judging her. So she said a silent prayer that God would somehow intervene on this girl's behalf. She hoped Nicole would call her, but she wasn't sure she would ever see this beautiful girl again.

Kathleen sat cold, alone and ashamed. With a thick cloud of disgrace hovering over her head, she sat there telling herself she was doing the right thing. The nurse came in and said that the doctor had to come in and talk to her, and then she would go get Shirley. This nurse was a little nicer than the others had been. She smiled at her, touched her arm and told her it would all be over soon. The doctor came in. He was a friendly looking man. He looked like Santa Claus with his rosy red cheeks. Under the right circumstances she probably would have liked him. Nevertheless, today he was the enemy coming to steal a precious jewel from her. He looked at her, seemingly sizing her up as he looked over the top of his glasses. "My name is Dr. Monroe," he said and extended his hand out to her. Kathleen didn't bother to shake his hand. She just wanted to bypass all the introductions and get "It" over with. He asked her a series of questions, the same questions that were on the form she had just filled out for the second time.

"Okay, I need you to lie back and relax," he said. What a joke, she thought - lie back and relax.
Kathleen asked him to have the nurse call Shirley. The doctor again explained to her the policy, but after much protest, he nodded and radioed the nurse to get Shirley.

It seemed like it took them forever to come. Then the

41

nurse opened the door and directly on her heels was Shirley, who looked like she was ready to faint.

The doctor frowned when he looked through the paper work. "How far along did you say that you were," he asked. "I am about 14 weeks," she said, after a small pause. He looked at her belly and then back at the paper work. He took out a yellow and pink measuring tape and measured her belly. The crease in the middle of his eyeballs began to increase. "Hum. Kathleen, I am going to have to do an ultrasound to clarify the date of conception because you say that you are fourteen weeks, but your HCG levels say something different. I need to find which one of you is accurate," he said smiling. She thought his smile was meant to comfort her, but Kathleen was trembling. Her whole body was shaking. He had assured her that the screen would be turned and she would not be able to see the images. Lord, I'm scared. She prayed, "Please don't leave me. Forgive me, God, for what I am about to do."

Brian looked down at his half-eaten food on his plate and sighed. It was good to have a home-cooked meal. He hadn't eaten too much of anything lately since he had left the house. Gwendolyn had made a big rib eye steak. It was okay, but not really seasoned the way he liked it. Yet, with A1 sauce it was pretty good. She had also made a huge baked potato with all the trimmings. He wasn't really a fan of potatoes either nor the little snow peas, but he really couldn't be picky. He was just glad to have a home-cooked meal. After all, she was trying her best to make him feel cozy, but something about the way she was looking at him made him want to run.

He remembered how Shirley had warned him about Gwendolyn. She was a lot smarter than he had thought. His instincts had told him she was an over-protective wife but now he was beginning to think she was right. This woman was after him, and just for a moment he was enjoying the attention. It had been a while since another woman had looked at him like she wanted him. He wanted to enjoy this just for a moment. "I can stop it at any time," he said to himself as he gazed at her lustfully.

Chamber two

Gwendolyn could tell she was wearing him down. He was softening, she laughed to herself. She had that effect on most men. She had no intentions of going over invoices. She had every intention of getting her way. She excused herself and went to the bathroom. She slipped into a sexy red dress, which perfectly accentuated her curves. She reapplied her makeup, sprayed some perfume and returned, only stopping to dim the lights and turn on the music. She was pleasantly surprised to see that he had poured two glasses of wine. He smiled when he saw her, and she sauntered over and sat next to him on the sofa. "So tell me, Mr. Hopkins, tell me what you desire," she purred.

Brian was intrigued by her beauty. She had beautiful ebony-toned skin. She was dark and lovely. She had long flowing hair that was naturally curly. It hung midway her back, and she was curved just right. Her big beautiful eyes were almost a bronze color with a blue ring around the outside of the pupil. He could see how she had men tending to her every beck and call. He couldn't believe that he had never noticed how beautiful she was before tonight. She smelled so good. It was almost like the aroma drifted up his nostrils and turned the logic button off in his brain because he could do nothing but drift deeper into this beautiful woman's gaze. Everything in him was telling him that this was going too far. Brian had to admit he was in a trance captured by her spell. He didn't want to end the night. Logic was outweighed this time. He didn't care about the consequences as he felt his manhood awaken. Something inside of him hungered. He just wanted to have her. No, he desperately needed to have her. His heartbeat quickened as she leaned in and kissed him first behind his right ear and then moved her tongue, flicking it as she worked her way toward his mouth. She teased the corners of his mouth building up excitement as she maneuvered her way down his chest. She unbuttoned his shirt with her tongue, and he gasped with contentment. Just for a moment, he was lost in a sea of pleasure. It felt as if he was in a dream. Everything happened in slow motion. She stood up, swaying to the music.

Her body swayed, tantalizing his senses as his heart began to pound harder. She stood up and unzipped her dress as she let it plummet to the floor leaving her black baby doll lingerie exposed. He could tell she had confidence in her body as her eyes twinkled playfully at him. She sat down on his lap, allowing her legs to straddle him. He couldn't help but reach up and grab her hips as she pressed her body into his first in a slow rhythmic motion, then feverously as she reached down to unbutton his pants.

"Oh no," he prayed. "Lord, you are going to have to help me." As if on cue, the phone rang startling him, snapping him out of this fantasy he was having and into reality.

Gwendolyn begged him not to answer the phone, but the fantasy was over. The truth was he was about to take advantage of this woman, knowing he did not love her and could never love her. He picked up the phone and on the other end of the line it was somebody trying to sell him a vacuum. He politely declined, took an exasperated breath and hung up the phone. Brian said a silent prayer to God because he knew that God had saved him once again. Brian turned to Gwendolyn; "I'm so sorry," he said. "I can't do this, not to you or to my wife." She sat there looking at him like he was a fool. At first she had tried to cajole him by whispering sweet nothings in his ear. Brian tried to make her understand. He tried to tell her that if he slept with her, then it would be a lie. He told her that she deserved a man that was going to love her, value her and give her the life she deserved. Brian wasn't sure she was listening to anything he said, but he hoped something he said got through to her.

Gwendolyn looked at him talking about how she deserved love. What did he know about her? What right did he have to judge her? He wanted her as much as she wanted him. She saw that look in his eyes.

She proceeded to tell him that he didn't know what he was talking about. She used to believe she was beautiful and loved. Yet, all that had changed one day when her mother's boyfriend, Shawn, had walked in on her while she was taking a shower. He didn't touch her, but he had looked at her and then turned around and left. Over the next couple of days he would just stare at her with a little smile on his face as he licked his lips. She knew what he was thinking about even though she was only twelve.

Then one day when her mother had to work late, her worst fears were confirmed. He came in drunk, snatched her by her pony tail, forced her into her mother's room, over-powered her, and made her have oral sex with him. After it was all over, he left her lying in her mother's bed, wounded and crying, and telling her that no one would ever love her. He continued violating her until one day he made her have intercourse with him. She was confused. She hated him; yet, her body still responded to his touches.

She felt disgusted and ashamed. She could still see herself laying there, shutting her eyes. She would shut her eyes so tight that tears would not escape. She had become a master of disembodiment. Gwendolyn had gotten the courage to talk to her mom after her best friend Max had told her that either she was going to tell or he was going to tell. "You can't let Shawn get away with what he's doing to you," he said as he wiped the tears from her eyes. "She's your mother. She has to know you would not lie about something like this!" he said. She had confided in Max only after she had found out she was pregnant. She was only fifteen, and she was scared out of her mind. She needed him to give her the money to get the abortion. He had insisted on knowing who the father was. He was shocked when she had told him the truth. Max was the only person who had ever given a hoot about her. He was her only friend in the world. They had been neighbors as long as she could remember. He gave her the money and went with her to get the abortion after she had promised to tell her mother the truth.

She could still remember that day. She unlocked the door after school, hung up her backpack on the rusted nail in the wall and walked into the kitchen, smelling the aroma of meatloaf and apple pie, two smells that she hated even to this day. Her mother was sitting at the kitchen table watching her favorite soap opera as she peeled potatoes. She slipped past her as her stomach ached. It had been three days since the abortion, but the pains in her stomach intensified.

Gwendolyn thought that if she lay down for a little bit, she would be okay, but she dozed off to sleep. She was awakened by the feeling of something wet and sticky between her legs. She was horrified to find out that it was blood. She yelled for her mother in a panicked voice. Her mother stumbled in the room and found her unconscious. Her mother rushed her to the hospital. When she finally came to, she heard the doctor, her mom and Shawn talking. The doctor told them she was lucky to be alive! The doctor who had performed the procedure left part of the placenta inside her. They were informed that she would have to stay for a little while to get rid of the infection, and he wanted to keep an eye on her to make sure no other complications would arise. He told her, "You are a lucky young lady. A few more hours and you would have been dead." He left her alone with her mother who was now playing the role of the distraught mother. That quickly dissipated when she began to tell her the story. She was not surprised at her mother's response although it tore a wall in her heart that has forever been void since that day.

Her mother told her how disappointed she was in her. She had taught her to always tell her the truth. She told her she was just an ungrateful slut and was trying to ruin any happiness for her life because she hated Shawn. Her mother accused her of fabricating the whole story. She would not even listen to her, so she admitted to her mom that she had kissed him and sat on his lap and that was all that had happened. She had admitted that it was all her enticing him. Another lie to hide the secret no one really wanted to hear. Then Gwendolyn told her that Max was the baby's dad.

Shawn stood there, looking at her, mocking her as he assured her mom that he had done nothing wrong and that Gwendolyn was like every other teenager with "overactive hormones." "It was quite normal," he had said. What did he know about normal? Her life had not been close to normal since he had become a part of her life. Even though her mom refused to admit it, she was sure her mother knew what was going on.

Max's dad was not happy when Gwendolyn's mother told him about the abortion, and Max had never told anyone the truth either. She later found out that his dad had shipped him off to boarding school. Gwendolyn was sure that Max hated her because he had never contacted her after that day. Who could blame him?

Shawn continued raping her until she was sixteen. One day when she came home from school, he was sitting there waiting for her. He tried to force himself on her. Only this time she was ready. She grabbed the switchblade from her backpack and fought back. She swung wildly with her eyes closed. She stabbed him in his leg and his arm. The blood gushed out from the wounds. He swore and doubled over in pain. He told her that she was his now and nobody would want her. He told her that her mother was going to hate her when he told her what she had done and how she had wanted him. She ran into her room, threw whatever she could fit into her backpack, and grabbed the money out of her tin can bank and her mom's petty cash, which they had been saving for a vacation. She ran away and never looked back since.

She lived on the streets and in halfway houses for a while, and then when she was seventeen, she had met a man named George who was nice. He helped her get a place and a job, and they dated three years; they even contemplated getting married. She was so happy. Then she found out he had a wife and three kids! He had told her he was twenty-four when he was actually thirty-one. Gwendolyn found out a few months later that his name wasn't even George; it was Johnny. So, she was left once more alone. Gwendolyn had tears streaming down her face. She listened as he apologized profusely for almost being like all the other men she had been with. She hurried up, grabbed her stuff and left, feeling dirty and used.

~

Shirley listened to the doctor and then prayed to herself, "God I know this is You. Lord, I don't know what You are doing, but if You need me, I am available."

The doctor told Shirley that she would have to wait outside either in the lobby or outside the door. He said it should be a pretty quick look and then they would start the procedure. He also told her she would not be allowed inside the room for the procedure, but he would allow her to come in briefly beforehand. Shirley was frustrated as she waited outside the room while they began the ultrasound. What was going to happen? "Oh Lord, teach me to wait on You. I trust You." She paced the hallway and then as if a force was compelling her to the room. Shirley found herself opening the door.

She saw Kathleen lying on the table with her eyes tightly closed as if she was trying to imagine herself anywhere but here. Shirley was drawn to the images on the screen. The baby looked like it was fully formed. She saw its head, and there were little lines on the bottom of the screen indicating the baby's heartbeat. The doctor looked up and motioned to the nurse. She walked over to Shirley and told her she needed to leave the room. "No one is allowed in here except the patient," said the nurse. She also informed Shirley that if she caused any problems, she would have the security guard remove her from the premises. Shirley knew she had to do something. The nurse had radioed for security when Shirley had said she was not leaving. The nurse had actually tried to physically remove her from the room. Shirley planted her feet and in the tussle grabbed the screen as she almost toppled over. Then they heard it…. the heartbeat somewhere in the struggle. The speaker had been turned on and they heard it. Baaboom, Baaboom. The heartbeat thumped, filling the room. The doctor tried to maneuver the screen to shield it from Kathleen. He turned the speaker off, but it was too late. Kathleen was sitting up on the table, staring at the screen.

Kathleen stared at the screen. It was a baby! Her baby! She looked at the doctor in horror as she thought about what she was about to do. She was going to kill her baby.

"My God!" She said over and over again, tears flowing down her face. Her sobs began to echo in the room dissipating through the hallways.

The doctor took an exaggerated breath and asked her if she needed to take some time to get herself together. He threw a disapproving look at the nurse, who continued to glare at Shirley. Shirley was oblivious to anything happening around her. She sat looking at Kathleen, knowing that God had just performed the miracle she had been praying for. Tears poured down her face as she saw the look of recognition on her friend's face as she realized the baby on the screen was real, not just a bunch of dividing cells. Shirley still wasn't sure what was going through Kathleen's mind, but she knew that she would not be able to deny the baby she was carrying.

"Kathleen, I would like to finish the ultrasound," said Dr. Monroe. "Then I can talk to you a little more and explain the procedure. Okay? Would you like a little time to regroup?" he asked. Kathleen nodded yes and laid back, her eyes still glued to the screen.

Shirley could look at the doctor and tell that he was uncomfortable, but he did well to keep his professionalism. He left quickly. She could tell he was glad to be out of the room. The nurse gratefully followed. She heard him greet another patient and close the door behind him.

"Kat, are you okay?" Shirley asked. After what seemed like an eternity, Kathleen finally spoke. "Shirley," she said. "I'm so glad you are here Shirley. I just don't know what to say." She lay there looking at the ceiling.

Shirley began to pray, "Lord, I know that You intervened on Kathleen's behalf, but now speak to her as only You can. Reassure her that You have not left her nor forsaken her. You are her help and her hiding place. Thank You, Lord. Help her see that this baby is a blessing.

Replace her fear with joy and boldness, so that she will know that you will be her refuge. Hallelujah, Jesus!" she said as she danced around the small room. She danced for Kathleen.

Her friend needed a breakthrough, and if she needed to open the gates of heaven with her praise, she was going to give God a stupid praise. Shirley felt overwhelming joy and in the midst of her prayer, God spoke a word for her own life. He promised her that Brian would return and that everything the enemy had stolen from her would be returned double. He assured her that nothing happened without His knowledge. Just like Job who had everything taken away and looked like he was down and out, God called him "righteous". And the very thing that Satan tried to destroy him with, God used for His glory. He promised that the road would be long and hard and sometimes overwhelming, but He said He would never leave her nor forsake her. Fear not, for He was with her. It was almost in a small whisper, but when she heard Him speak, she was grateful. Shirley loved the Lord, and now she knew that He loved her. God was real and He was still on the throne. He knew the plans that He had for her. She was going to do her best to line her will up with God's will so that His divine purpose would be fulfilled in her life.

Kathleen lay there, watching her friend Shirley dancing around the room like a wild woman. That girl was crazy! She had what most people thought of as ridiculous faith. It seemed like nothing for her to believe in things most people would have given up on a long time ago. She suddenly realized how blessed she was to have Shirley even though her methods were often considered rambunctious to most people. Kathleen knew that Shirley loved her and despite her stubbornness, her friend had been an intricate part of stopping her from ruining her life and killing her baby. She sobbed quietly at first, then she felt a pressure building up inside. When she reached her climax, she let go her emotions riveting to and fro. She called out to God. When she could cry no more, she laid back on the table, waiting for the doctor to come. So many questions bombarded her mind. How was she going to raise this baby? What kind of life would she provide? She knew there was no way she could go through with the abortion, but she still didn't know what God wanted from her. She and Danny had tried so hard to have a baby. And it was ironic now that she was pregnant; he was not here to share any of it with her. Life was so unfair. They had been through three miscarriages in their twelve-year marriage. Now that she was pregnant, how was she going to do it by herself? She felt unsure about her future. She felt like she was schizophrenic because she was going through so many emotions all at once. Kathleen wasn't sure of many things any more, but she was sure of one thing: this baby was coming, and she needed to figure out what to do. She was comforted by a familiar small whisper saying, "The battle is not yours, Kathleen. I will never leave you or forsake you." As quick as it came, it left. She realized that she was going to have to take one thing at a time, and right now she needed to get through the ultrasound.

Brian hadn't seen Gwendolyn since the night she left. He wondered if she was still mad. He hadn't talked to Shirley lately although she had called. He had not returned her calls. He didn't know what to say. Brian knew that Shirley's mind worked in the black and white technical aspect of things. To her, he already had an affair even though it never reached sex, but just allowing someone else in the space he and Shirley shared only with each other was unforgivable to her.

His mind began to have a conversation of its own,

"good" versus "bad". "You guys are separated. There is no need to tell her anything. You know if you tell her, she will never take you back," said Bad. "Are you kidding? She loves you. She will forgive you because love conquers all," answered Good. "Don't believe that lie. You left her, remember? You told her that you didn't love her.... so she won't believe you! She will think that Gwendolyn was the reason you left!" said Bad. "And anyway, how do you cheat on someone you are not with?" asked Bad.

"No way! Don't believe that! God is truth, and He has promised to never leave you or forsake you. He has promised to be faithful and to forgive you. Just ask for forgiveness, and He will touch her heart. What God has put together, no man can put a severance to," concluded Good. Then his stomach had that bilious feeling, so he lay down on the couch. Did he really want to save his marriage? He knew that he still loved her. What did he really want? He loved her, but was that really enough? Look at what love had done to Danny and Kathleen.

It was almost as if Kathleen would have been better off never having met Danny. At least she would not have had a broken heart. Whoever said, "It's better to have loved and lost than never to have loved at all"? It leaves a rift in your spirit so large that nothing could ever replace it. What he wanted he didn't know, but nothing seemed the same without her. It was almost as if his passion was gone. He used to enjoy taking pictures. It was like he found the perfect moment, and then it was captured, suspended in time but never forgotten. His work had earned him numerous awards and was on display in numerous galleries. Lately, he had been very distracted, and it showed in his work. He looked at the clock and saw that it was 7:00pm and his stomach began to growl. He still hadn't gone grocery shopping, so Brian decided to go to his favorite Italian restaurant. His life may be falling apart, but at least tonight he would eat well.

Gwendolyn hadn't really done much of anything lately since her encounter with Brian. She wasn't sure if it was the fact that he had rejected her or the indignant look he gave her as he sat there looking at her, pretending that he even had a clue of anything about her. "You deserve someone to love you", he had said. Boy, he had really pissed her off and she had every intention of letting him know exactly how she felt the next time she saw him. He had made her relive her past every day since that night. And he wasn't bothering to even answer the phone when she called. Yes, he was going to pay her the funky money he owed her, too. "I should call his wife," she thought to herself, but then she thought some women tend to get aggressive when it comes to their men. Even though Shirley seemed like one of those crazy Christians, one thing Gwen had learned was that everyone who claimed to be "saved" wasn't stable. And here she was sitting in church and wondering how did she get duped into coming here. She had one lady at work, Linda, who kept bothering her about going to church with her. She'd promised to go, although she never had any intention of going for real.

After Linda kept bugging her; she thought she would really go just to shut her up. It wasn't all that bad. She sat there listening to the music as the choir sang; she could get with this. Gwen loved music. It was her only avenue out of her horrible life. When she was a kid, she would turn her earphones up so loud to drown out the sounds of her everyday hell. You know the screaming, the cussing, the slamming and the banging of everyday life. The song they were singing was the most beautiful song she had ever heard. The lyrics rang repeatedly in her head

"Nothing that I've done, nothing I could ever do, could take me from the presence of Your hand that's holding me."

"Wow, whoever wrote this song definitely didn't know me." Gwendolyn said a little too loud. Yet it was the truth. She was the exception to every rule. God didn't love her. In fact, she would be pretty certain that to Him, she was invisible. He was busy with other people. When it came to her, God could never seem to be found. If He indeed loved her, then why didn't He protect her from the horrid thing she called life?

Then the stares started. First, from the older women whom they called the church mothers although they didn't seem very nurturing. Then, this lady in front of her kept staring at her. I mean, turning around looking dead in her face. She didn't have the nerve to pretend to look at something else. There was a young couple directly beside her. The husband looked no more than about 19 and the wife maybe 18, at the most. Gwen nearly fell out of her seat when the husband leaned forward and winked at her. His wife didn't appreciate this little exchange and glared at her. Gwen at first felt uncomfortable but then laughed to herself as the young girl grabbed her husband and laid her head against his shoulder. "He's not my type anyway," she thought, as she peeped at his olive green suit and navy blue socks. He was a "kid" who didn't present too much of a challenge for Gwen. Besides, he wouldn't be able to handle her. She would have sent him back to his Mama traumatized. Why was it that trouble seemed to follow her wherever she was? Here she was in church minding her own business, and it had found her already. She was not a person most people had a split opinion about. She was either liked or hated.

Almost as if Linda sensed her uneasiness, she reached

out and grabbed her hand and smiled as the preacher took the pulpit and began to bring the word. She sat there captivated by her confidence as she spoke. Gwen was a little taken aback to see that the pastor was a woman. She had never heard of a woman pastor, but when this woman took the pulpit, it was almost as if she was talking directly to Gwen. She told the story of the prodigal son and while in the pigpen, he realized he was in the mess. Oh, but when he remembered who he was and went back to his father's house, his father met him in the field and received him back. This lady brought the word through everyday life examples, which made it so easy to listen to. Gwendolyn had never heard the gospel preached like this. She felt something happening. Her stomach was filled with butterflies, and she suddenly felt like a warm wet blanket was placed around her shoulders. Even though there weren't but about sixty people in the room, you would have thought that the whole auditorium was packed to full capacity. This lady preached so hard that her earrings went flying across the floor. The next thing she knew, the pastor's shoes were gone and she was dancing so hard she looked like she would pass out.

Gwen found herself standing up and suddenly she was in the middle of aisle dancing, too. Tears began to run down her face. "I don't know what you want from me, God!" she screamed. People began to turn around and look at her, and a couple people seemed annoyed.

Gwen only knew one thing. She couldn't leave the same way she came. Did God really want her? Was he drawing her or was she still the exception to every rule? "Lord, if it's really You, please show me that You love me and I will serve You," she prayed. She was blinded by her tears. "Lord, I need you, but I don't know what you want me to do. I just know that I can't do it by myself. I need you!" she screamed. Which, of course, turned more heads, but Gwen was tired of running. She was tired of masks she had worn, so many masks that she didn't know who she really was. She was tired of her life, and she wanted peace. She was determined not to leave here without hearing from God.

The pastor walked down the aisle and stopped directly in front of Gwen. She took her hand and placed it over her heart and told her that God loved her. He wanted to use her, but He would not force His way in. He wanted her to invite Him in. She also told her she didn't have to run anymore. That she was unique to God and eyes had not seen and ears had not heard the plans for her life. God had sent her here to receive her healing if she would let Him. It was almost as if an earthquake happened in her soul, and everything in her began to fall apart. It literally felt like the inside of her was cracking. She felt her body begin to get warm almost as if she was running a temperature. She heard the pastor whisper in her ear, "Let him work. He is healing you emotionally."

God had set her up all this time. She had thought she was misplaced when really God had invited her to have an encounter with Him. She felt overwhelming joy penetrate her heart, and she laughed for the first time in years. It came deep from within her belly. She couldn't stop laughing if she tried and she couldn't stop crying. She was so confused. Through her tears something happened. Some sort of release took place…. she cried for the young girl inside of her that just wanted to be loved. She cried for her baby that she never knew….she cried for the things she never allowed herself to think about because the pain was too great. She cried for the woman that she had become. And the woman she didn't know how to be. She cried out to God, "Take it." She pleaded through her tears, and this time she really meant it. She tired of trying to do it her way. She needed Him to do it for her. And there was nothing or no one that could take this moment away from her. It was almost as if she personally was ushered into the throne room of God and for the first time she knew He was listening. She found herself being led step by step. It was as if the constraints of time could not hinder the crossing of the parallel universes as she met her destiny. She was being guided toward the front of the church, barely able to see past her tears. She stumbled. The pastor held her hand and together they walked, each connected. Despite their walking different paths, they were forever linked by this encounter with God as He called her by name.

Gwendolyn stood there in front of the church filled with people, and her tears asked Jesus to be the Lord of her life. "Imagine that," she thought. Her makeup was smeared, her dress was hanging every which way, and she looked a hot mess, but she had never looked prettier. Gwendolyn knew that because she had met God, and He had introduced himself as the father that she never had. He really loved her, and for the first time she felt happy. It was real.

Kathleen stared at the ultrasound pictures. It was a girl. She could not believe that she was having a girl. Looking at the pictures, she felt so overwhelmed. She had almost killed her baby girl. The realization that there was a little life that she was going to be responsible for began to set in. I'm going to be somebody's mommy. She said over and over again as the thought began to settle into her being.

The doctor had surprised her by telling her that going by the ultrasound; she was almost twenty-three weeks pregnant. Her blood work had also confirmed the findings of the ultrasound. She looked at them dumbfounded as she sat there and tried to go back in her mind to understand how she was eight weeks more pregnant than what she thought. The nurse had seemed annoyed when she had changed her mind about the abortion. The nurse was not happy with Shirley, and she had no problem letting her know by the look on her face. The doctor had said that he would not have been able to perform the abortion anyway, at this particular clinic. They only did them up to seventeen weeks, but he did give a list of other providers who did abortions on into the second trimester and a list of providers of OB doctors just "in case" he said with a twinkle in his eye. He also advised her to talk to a grief counselor, saying that it would help her sort through things. He gave her a card, saying this person was very reliable and a friend of his. The day she had been dreading was over. It was just like all the stress and buildup of weeks of worry and depression were gone. She was going to have a baby girl. She still wasn't ready to run out and tell the world, but for right now she felt a little excitement building up.

Shirley stood in her best friend's house, painting the baby's room. She wasn't really sure where Kathleen's mind had been lately. She seemed like she was getting better, but she had her good days and her bad days. She had left a while ago to see the counselor. She seemed to really like him. And Kathleen had even gone back to work. She was a novelist, and was working on a pretty big project, which she was trying to finish before the baby came. They had found out that the baby was due in October, 16 to be exact, and there was so much left do. With Kathleen pretty busy these days, it left Shirley alone a lot, and she threw herself into projects for the baby.

Shirley stepped back to look at her masterpiece. It had taken her a while, but the room looked fabulous. She had painted the walls a light yellow and had chosen the theme of Peter Cottontail, so she painted decals of little cottontail bunnies hopping down a bunny trail. It was darling if she had to say so herself.

Shirley was so thrilled that Kathleen was going to have the baby. And she was even more ecstatic when she found out it was a girl. Yet a few days earlier as she was thinking back over the events that had transpired; she felt a little twinge of jealousy begin to creep into her thoughts. If there was one thing Shirley knew, she didn't need to give the devil any room in her life. She was trusting God for the things too big for her. Things only God could do. She was not about to let a little bit of jealousy keep her from her blessings, so she quickly asked God to remove the twinge she felt and replace it with joy. Before long, the feeling had disappeared. She was planning the baby shower list and tomorrow, she was going to get the crib.

She picked up the cell phone and instinctively dialed Brian's number. She wanted to hang up as she heard the phone begin to ring, but it was too late. He answered, "Now, what do I do?" she exclaimed to herself. It was almost as if she had lost all reason. She felt like a little school girl with her stomach in knots. And with the little composure she had she said, "Hello" and paused, listening for his reply. "Hello, yourself," he said. She paused a little, not sure why she had even called him. Just knowing something deep inside her wanted to hear his voice. No, something needed to hear his voice. "Brian, we need to talk," she said, breaking the awkward silence. "I know," he said. "I miss you." She could almost see the expression on his face, and she could hear the pain in his voice. She counted to ten before she responded; after all, she did not want to appear desperate. "Me too, Brian, but one thing I've been asking myself is how did we get here?" she said. "I don't know," he said. His voice was transparent. It had a childlike innocence, and she knew he really had no idea.

One thing was certain: he still had feelings for her.

~

They agreed to meet at his house tonight for dinner where they could sit down and talk. "What would you like - Mexican or Chinese? You know I don't cook," he said with a laugh. It was good to hear him laugh. It seemed like forever. Her heart began to get that familiar feeling, and she felt the longing to be near him. She hadn't realized how much she missed him, the smell of his musk cologne and his ability to know what she was thinking before she finished the sentence. She had always felt so safe with him. He would wrap his arms around her, and it was as if her soul united with his. Sometimes, she would lay her head down on his chest and listen to his heart as it beat in time with hers, synchronized in their own rhythm. "Mexican," she answered, her eyes filling with tears. She wanted to say so much more, but it would have to wait until tonight. She would tell him everything that was in her heart. She was tired of playing it safe. She wanted him home. He was her husband, and she was tired of playing games. Shirley hung up the phone and turned around almost bumping into Kathleen.

"So what's going on?" Kathleen demanded. "What you talking about?" asked Shirley, as if she didn't know what she was talking about. "You have been spending all your time at my house. You know what I'm talking about! You know you don't like me that much. Don't you dare try to play me," Kathleen said and playfully punched her in the arm. "What is the deal? What is going on with you and Brian?"

Shirley looked at Kathleen and knew that she couldn't prolong the inevitable anymore. She needed to face the news herself. "Brian moved out," she said and casually tried to change the subject with caution. "Do you like the room?" she said. "What did you say? And don't you dare try to change the subject," said Kathleen.

"Brian moved out. He said he wasn't in love with me anymore," she said softly almost as if she didn't have enough air to finish the sentence. "He moved out! Where is he living?" Kathleen asked. "He rented an apartment about twenty minutes away," she whispered. It was almost as if she was afraid of saying the words out loud. Then it would mean that she acknowledged the issue, and it could no longer go undetected. She blinked quickly, hoping to discourage tears from escaping her eyes. She trusted God, but for just a brief moment, she was scared. Petrified that Brian just might be gone for good, and the thought of losing the only man she had ever loved was a little more than she could deal with at the present moment. She was not about to let herself fall apart. She needed to keep busy, so she scanned the room quickly looking for something to focus her attention on. She spotted a laundry basket of clothes and tried to keep busy fixating on folding the little shirts and jeans she had bought for the baby.

Kathleen looked at her friend. She was falling apart. She remembered how it felt the night she had gotten a phone call by an obviously shaken Brian, telling her that there had been an accident. A drunk driver had hit them head on in a police pursuit. It was really bad. The scene had happened only minutes away from his exit. She blindly pulled herself out of bed and threw on Danny's oversized shirt. It was his favorite, and she still slept with it today.

She had pulled on her jeans and hurried to the scene. It looked like a street full of mangled metal where the SUVs

had collided. The smoke was still permeating the air. Cars were whizzing by on the opposite side of the highway, unaware of the tragedy that had just happened.
People were everywhere. Blue and red lights from the emergency vehicles were flashing as they shut down the highway for hours.

Brian was banged up pretty bad although his injuries were not considered life threatening. His body had recovered, but emotionally he had never recovered from that day. Danny, on the other hand, was really hurt. They weren't sure if he was going to make it.

She remembered the panic that had filled Shirley's voice when she had told her that Brian and Danny had been in an accident. This was the only time that she had ever seen her friend lose control. It was a long wait. It seemed like an eternity as she and Shirley sat clinging to each other as they waited for word. It was Shirley who quickly recovered and kicked into operation savior mode; organizing, making the phone calls and pestering the doctors for information. The doctor had come out and reassured them that the guys were doing okay. He turned his attention to Kathleen and told her she could go in and see Danny, but he needed to talk to her first, and the nurses needed her to fill out some forms.

He was hooked to a ventilator, and he looked so frail. This was the man who had always been her source of strength. He opened his eyes when she walked into the room. She could see he was struggling to say something, but the ventilator prevented his words from being audible. Instead, the clinking and clanking of the machine resonated throughout the room.

He seemed to recognize her, as she leaned in and kissed him on the cheek. She saw his muscles tense and she told him to relax, everything would be okay.

The doctor motioned for her to step out of the room. He

told her that there had been a bruise on his liver, one of his lungs had collapsed from the explosion of the airbag in his car, and he needed to do surgery as soon as possible; but his chances were good, that he would fully recover. She signed the necessary paperwork. Everything happened so fast. She struggled to even fit in a breath long enough to replenish the oxygen that was quickly escaping from her body.

She said a prayer with Danny, kissed him on his forehead, and he was gone. That was the last time she saw him alive. The doctor said that during surgery, his other lung collapsed and he had a stroke and died on the operating table. And just like that he was gone; everything had been a blur since that day. She had often asked herself, "If she had known she would never see him again, what would she have done differently? What would she have said? Would she have even said a word or would she have just embraced him one last time memorizing the moment she would say goodbye to her soul mate?" She had sat hours in the green room at the hospital listening to the grief counselors talk to her about healing a wound they never could imagine.

Shirley once again took charge, arranging for the hospital to take Danny's body to the funeral home and contacting their closest friends. Kathleen was so incoherent that she didn't know one day from the next. The days following his death, Kathleen sat dazed. It was Shirley who made all the funeral arrangements. Shirley had even picked out his suit. Somehow, she thought that if she could deny his death, then she could hold on to him. Now she realized the only way she could live, was to let him die.

She felt her baby stir inside of her. The butterflies she had felt at first had long been replaced with lively movements, assuring her that she was carrying a life deep inside her. Through their daughter, Danny would live on. She was blessed to have a piece of him still left.

Right now Shirley needed her help. Kathleen knew that she had been kinda out of it lately, but right now she needed to get it together. "Suck it up and move on," as Shirley would have said. She looked at her friend and suddenly she had a surge of strength. In the past, Shirley may have been the one to have all the right answers, but today it was her turn to help her friend. There was one problem. She didn't have the right answer, nor did she know the place to start. She was sure of one thing; Brian was in for one heck of a fight. Whether or not he acknowledged it, Shirley was the best thing that ever happened to him, and their marriage was worth saving.

Brian hung up the phone. He missed her so much, but his love for her had never been a question for him. He needed to know that he was a priority in her life and not just another project. People were always having emergencies and Shirley always felt the need to get involved and smooth out their lives. Tonight it would be nice to just talk. He couldn't help but feel excited. Maybe tonight would bring new possibilities. Of what, he had no clue, but he really wanted to go back home; just not to the same marriage he left.

When he first moved out, he thought that he may have been overreacting, and maybe he was running away because of insecurities. It was true - Danny's death had been a difficult thing for him to swallow, but right now, this was much bigger than the panic he had felt when he had first moved out. Brian had to admit, although being away from her was torture, staying with her would have been worse. He couldn't keep pretending that everything was okay; Shirley never really dealt with anything in her life. She was a wonderful woman, and an even better lover, but she did not know how to be his wife.

After the death of their daughter, Shirley did what she always does. She started a crusade raising awareness for preterm labor due to an incompetent cervix. She had even made little brochures and handed them out at several doctor offices and hospitals. Of course, from that sprung a support group for grieving families, which took up most of her time. All this was not entirely bad; however, there was one problem. Shirley never allowed herself to grieve. Brian always seemed to be the farthest down the list of her priorities. "Well, we don't have to solve everything tonight" he thought to himself. At least they could talk, and he was glad for that.

Chamber three

Gwendolyn and Linda had been pretty close since she had joined the church, and she was feeling great. In fact, Linda had insisted on taking her out to celebrate her new "birthday in Christ". Linda truly was one of the sweetest women she knew; plus, she really believed in Gwen. She saw something no one had ever bothered to look for. Gwen hated that it had taken her so long to get to know her; after all, they had worked together for three years. Until recently, Linda had virtually been a stranger.

Her cell phone rang. It was Robin. She was her road dog and her best friend. They had been through a lot together, the good and the bad. Although she loved Robin, she had been avoiding her lately. Gwendolyn realized her life was changed now and the drama that once excited her, now made her sick to her stomach. "Well," she thought, "I can't hide forever." She picked up the phone.

"Hello", she said dryly, hoping to keep the conversation short and sweet. "Girl, where you been?" said Robin seemly unaware of Gwen's irritation. She continued, rambling on -- not stopping to even take a breath. "I saw Brian's wife yesterday. Girl, what is really going on?" Gwen didn't respond.

"You trippin'! So you're holding back, huh? Are you gonna tell a sista what's really going down or what?!" Robin stopped, finally, pausing to get a breath.

Gwendolyn quickly interjected, hoping to divert the conversation away from Brian. "Girl, it's been crazy. You know I joined the church a few weeks ago, and things have been busy."

"Yea, I heard" said Robin grimly. "So, whatcha sayin'? Now you saved and sanctified and don't have no time for the hoodlums of the world, right?"

"Robin, you know that is not fair; I'm just trying to live right. I've done so much wrong in my life that I need to get it right. Jesus died for me and my sins, and now I have a chance at a new life." Gwen said passionately.

"Don't you dare stick your nose up in the air and talk to me about Jesus. He don't care about people like us. You know… the home-wreckers. Have you forgotten? All your boyfriends have been married? What does your Jesus say about that?" Robin said with such anger, it sent chills down Gwendolyn's spine.

"Look, Robin, I didn't mean to imply I'm any better than you. I just wanted you to know that there is a Savior, and He died for us as well as anyone. I can't make you accept Him, but those who don't will spend eternity in hell. Now, some people don't believe in hell. I know one thing: I don't want to be the one to test the theory and see if it's real." said Gwendolyn.

It was Robin's turn to be silent, and after an awkward pause, Robin responded saying, "You are weaker than I thought. Jesus is for those crazy people who try to make themselves feel good by pretending that there is "some being" higher than them that actually cares whether they live or die. Girl, we are cut from the same cloth, and no amount of Jesus can change that. Gwen, it's been real; call me when you are not in denial anymore," she spewed and slammed down the phone.

Gwendolyn sat stunned as she kept hearing Robin's words echoing over and over in her head. The words stung as they began probing her heart as if they were looking for any opening to embed and take root. Out of all people, she thought her best friend would be happy she was getting her life together. "What did Robin know?" she said to herself. "She doesn't know anything about me." The real problem was that she knew too much about her, and the truth hurt. She had been all those horrible things, but she was different now. "I really have changed!" she said. She thought if she said it out loud she would believe it. Then a thought began to form, "What if Robin is right. What if you are not capable of changing?" It poised and lingered, opening the door for a trail of other questions. Then it began…the battle between today and yesterday. Only today wasn't quite as strong as the past, so it was quickly overtaken. Instantly, "yesterday" began to bombard her with thoughts. Gwen saw what she thought were shadows creeping into the room. Pretty soon it was as if they had swarmed her, and accusations continued to roll around in her head. She struggled to sit down on the couch, overtaken and afraid. The voices kept getting louder and louder, and pretty soon she felt consumed.

"You know she's right. You can't just recite a little prayer and everything is over just like that. Were you surprised? Did you think God would just forgive you and everything would instantly go away? Stop fooling yourself. You are what you are. Everybody can see that you are fooling yourself. You're not really changed; it was just a bunch of stupid emotions, anyway. You know you're not saved. What does the pastor know about Jesus loving you?

If she really knew you, she would know she was talking to the wrong person. People are still talking about you! They see through the hype into the real you; the rotten part of your soul that you think no one else sees. If they did, they would confirm what you know; you're not worthy of love."

Tears began to spill down her face. What if she was wrong? What if she really was fooling herself? Gwendolyn felt like everybody had decided about her and kept charging her with the same offenses over and over. What if she really was deceived and was really on her way to Hell? She knew that's where she deserved to go. "Lord, I know that You can make Yourself real to me if You want to. I need You to help me through this. I desperately want to know that I belong to You. Are You listening to me? I need You!" she pleaded.

The doorbell rang, and Gwen tried to pull herself together and come up with an excuse (she suddenly didn't feel like a celebrating mood). She opened the door, and Linda was standing there with an arm full of balloons that said Happy Birthday and Welcome to the family. "Girl, this house is beautiful!" said Linda as she entered her living room and thrust the balloon bouquet into her hands. She stood in the middle of the room as she took in the warmness of the colors. "Wow, you are really talented. You really should think about going into business for yourself. I'll volunteer to do your bookkeeping," she said. It wasn't until she turned around and saw the look on Gwen's face that she realized something was wrong. "What's the matter with you?" asked Linda. Gwendolyn thought about denying anything was wrong, but she needed help. So, she told her about the conversation. Linda listened intently, not interrupting one time. When Gwen finished, she was balling her eyes out, but she felt better. They sat there for a while, quiet.

Gwen was beginning to wonder if Linda was ever going to say anything at all. Then Linda finally cleared her throat and said, "Man, that's tough. I'm sorry you had to go through that. Sometimes, the people we think would be the most supportive are the ones that aren't. You know, Satan comes to kill, steal and destroy, and he doesn't care who he uses to do that. Gwen, you have to remember she is operating in the flesh, and the flesh cannot understand things of the Spirit. If a total stranger accused us, it wouldn't have as much impact as a family member or close friend." Gwen knew that Linda was right, but she still had doubts. "What if I'm not the person you think I am?"

stammered Gwen.

"What do you mean?" questioned Linda.

"What if the person you think that I am, is not who I am," asked Gwen.

"You don't need to worry what anyone else thinks about you. I was on drugs for fifteen years. I worked the streets selling my body and drugs. A woman came and witnessed to me, and she told me of this man named Jesus who had come to earth because he loved me. At first, I didn't think she knew what she was talking about, but this woman had a look that I had never seen. She was talking to me with so much love and compassion, by the time I finished talking with this woman of God, I felt like I could conquer the world. This woman came into the crack house and got me, so you can't tell me anything about not being worthy," explained Linda. "God found me, and He justified me, Gwen.

He came and gave me a worth that nobody can ever take away from me. That's what I see when I look at you. If God says you are worthy, who am I to say that you are not?" Linda spoke with so much passion that her voice shook with emotion. Gwen stared at her as Linda looked her square in her eye and said, "You may have a hard time understanding what I'm saying, but I am going to keep telling you God loves you. He doesn't care about what the world says. You have worth. God calls you His beloved. He will send someone wherever you are, and that person will speak into your spirit, and that is what I have been charged to do. You might not believe it, but I know it. Now, let's go celebrate your birthday in Christ!"

Gwendolyn looked at Linda, and as they walked out arm and arm, they held their heads up high. She said a silent prayer to God, thanking Him for a woman like Linda. She was not afraid to tell what God had delivered her from. The problem with most Christians was they make you think that they were born with a Bible in their hands and a "Hallelujah" on their lips; that you can never reach their level of "Holiness". It was cool to have someone who really knew who she was and wasn't afraid to reach back and help someone else. Man, one day I am going to be able to help someone else because of everything I've been through. Gwen thought the prospect was a little overwhelming now. Maybe one day she would turn around and someone else would be holding on to her with the same terrified look her own face wore. Until then, she was going to hold on to Linda. She was excited because she knew they were headed on one heck of a journey.

Shirley heard her phone ringing just as she was about to leave the house to meet Brian. She almost didn't answer it because she was running late, but she went back anyway. Moments later she stood paralyzed with fear, trying to figure out who the panicked voice was on the phone. "I didn't know who else to call, I don't even know if you remember me". The voice said. "What's the matter?" asked Shirley. Her years of crisis counseling had taught her to keep the caller talking and to try to diffuse the crisis. She hoped asking questions would calm the voice down enough to understand who it was. Then she could figure out what was going on. There was a long silence, and Shirley was beginning to wonder if the caller was still on the phone.

Then she heard her quick short breathes resounding through the receiver. "This is Nicole," said the caller between muffled cries and inaudible words. Shirley's brain scrambled trying place the name with a face, and then she remembered Nicole was the young girl she had met in the abortion clinic. "Nicole, are you okay? What's the matter?" asked Shirley in slow, even tones; she had to keep herself from being swept up into the emotion. "I can't do this anymore!" cried Nicole. "Where are you?" questioned Shirley. She heard tussling in the background a door slamming and glass shattering; by then Nicole was hysterical. Shirley finally calmed her down and promised to meet her. She took the address down and hurried out the door. It was only when she reached Nicole's house that she remembered where she was originally headed. She pulled out her cell phone, but decided to call Brian later. She hoped that she could help Nicole and still make it to dinner. He would definitely be mad. "I'll have to make it up to him," she said to herself as she hurried out of her car and up to the front door of Nicole's house.

Nicole met her at the door with a suitcase weeping profusely. "I didn't know who else to call," she cried as her body trembled. Shirley helped her get into the car, popped the trunk and placed Nicole's suitcase inside. As she slammed it down, she said a short prayer because she could already see this was more than she could handle. They rode in silence; in fact, the only sound that could be heard was an occasional sniffle coming from Nicole's direction. This continued until Shirley finally broke the silence, asking her if there was somewhere she wanted to go. Shirley decided to take her to her house after she said there was nowhere she could go.

Once they were in the house Shirley made a big pitcher of pink lemonade. "What is going on?" she asked cautiously as she handed her a full glass. Nicole took a big gulp; you could almost hear it as it dropped to the bottom of her stomach. She took a deep breath and began telling her the twisted story of her life.

"After Miles found out that I was thinking about keeping the baby, he turned into at creep. He began beating me and rationing out my food. Today it was really bad; he said he was going to kill me and the baby because we jacked up his life. It just isn't right. I made a mistake in having sex, but I don't think it's fair to my baby if I kill it," she said, and began to weep all over again. "I just don't know what to do. Miles says he doesn't want this baby and he doesn't want me....he says that I need to move; I don't have anywhere to go! I called the shelter, and they said they don't have any beds. Maybe if I show up there, they might have someone not show up or something." She looked so tiny under the weight that she was carrying. "My parents threw me out when they found out I was pregnant and decided to keep my baby. They insisted that this baby was going to screw up my life. I think I might be the one to screw up its life. I am not capable of being anyone's mom! What am I going to do?"

"Well, the first thing you are going to do is finish drinking your lemonade, then you are going to take a bubble bath, put on some pajamas and then we are going to kick back and relax while I order some food for us. What do you want?" she asked as she reached into the cabinet and handed her a fluffy green towel. I could go for some Mexican." Shirley said as she looked at her clock and realized it was after 1:00 am. Where did the time go? She thought Brian would be fuming. She picked up the phone to call him, and hung-up when she heard his answering machine. She would try to explain to him later. Right now, she needed to help Nicole get settled. It would be nice to have someone around. Besides, it had been awhile since her house had seen any life. Shirley turned her attention to Nicole who was standing in the same spot holding the towel. "Don't worry. We will figure something out. Until then you can stay here. Is something wrong?" she asked (she saw the puzzled look on Nicole's face).

"Why would you do all this for me? You don't even know me." stammered Nicole. "The first time I saw you, I knew you were special," Shirley said with a smile, remembering how beautiful this young girl looked. "It's not by accident that we ran into each other at the clinic. God sent me to you! We are going to make sure you have a healthy baby. Now go take a bath."

As Nicole eased down into the roman tub filled with bubbles (soothing the bruises on her body), she felt hopeful for the first time in a long time. Maybe things weren't as bad as she thought! Maybe things were really going to work out.

Brian opened another bottle of champagne as he watched the wax burn on the candles he had lit hours ago. He checked his phone for the hundredth time; still no message, so against his better judgment he dialed her number. "Hello you have reached Shirley; I'm unavailable please leave a message." He hung up before he could hear the rest of the message. He finished the glass of champagne and laid down on his futon. He picked up the phone and called his friend Paul, who was also a lawyer and told him he was ready to file for the divorce. He hung up the phone and blew out the candle, which had melted down to nothing. He didn't bother putting up the foil containers that held the Mexican food that had long ago grown cold. It was almost as if a door had shut in his heart, and he wasn't sure if he was willing to open it again.

Kathleen stared at the blank screen on her computer. She had been sitting there for almost three hours and nothing; she felt frustrated, she was behind schedule, and it seemed like she wasn't going to experience a breakthrough anytime soon. She decided to have some toast and then go for a little walk as the sun began to rise. She had to admit life seemed to get a little better. Richard, her therapist, said that's how coping began; you never forget them, you just learn how to cope without them. She welcomed the sunrays as they began to penetrate the night sky. She remembered how she used to hate to be reminded of another day.

Actually, she felt like she was coping quite well and she might just be able to be happy again. She knew Danny would have wanted that. Although sometimes she had really bad days but she was determined to get on with her life for her baby's sake. She reached her front porch and opened the door. As her stomach growled, she couldn't believe she was hungry again. She decided to call Shirley so she could take her to breakfast and see how her "date" with Brian went. "Hello," said an obviously still sleeping Shirley. "Get up, get ready, we are going to breakfast!" she said, mimicking Shirley's usual cheery voice. She hung up the phone before Shirley could object and headed out the door. As she walked out, she caught her reflection in the hall mirror. She was undeniably pregnant, and she looked pretty good even though she had on her sweats. "I'm still gorgeous," she thought as she giggled and walked out the door.

Shirley moaned as she looked at the clock. It was 6:00 a.m.!! "Man," she thought as she yawned lazily, stretching her arms above her head. Then she felt the cold rush to her face; oh no, Brian! She grabbed the phone and dialed his number again; his answering machine came on now. She knew he was not answering on purpose, because even if he had to work today, he never left his house before 6:00 a.m. on Saturday. "Brian this is Shirley; please pick-up! Come on, I know you are there!" she pleaded. She knew she sounded desperate, but she didn't care; she just wanted to talk to him. After it was evident he wasn't going to pick up the phone, she hung up. She would have to swing by his place today. Surely, he knew that she hadn't just stood him up. He had to know it was something important. She heard Nicole stirring in the next room. She took a shower and got dressed. By that time, she heard Kathleen and Nicole laughing downstairs. She walked down the stairs and saw them standing next to each other both glowing with that expectant mother look.

"Lord, I want to have a baby". she said. Something deep inside her was longing to be filled with life again. They turned around and looked at her, almost as if she was intruding. "Do I need to go back upstairs?" Shirley said with a laugh. "You guys need to be alone?"

"Not if you want to live! We are hungry." Kathleen giggled.

"I guess you have met each other?" Shirley asked. They both nodded. "Don't believe anything Kathleen says about me; she is a drama queen."

"Too late!" cackled Nicole, "She already filled me in on the gory details."

"What do you guys want for breakfast?" asked Kathleen. "I don't want to intrude on you guys," said Nicole. "After all, I just finished a bowl of cereal, and I could use some time to unpack."

Shirley looked at Kathleen and could tell from her raised eyebrow that she had questions for her. "Alright," Shirley responded, "We won't be gone long. You know my cell phone number. Don't hesitate to call if you need me, Nicole." Shirley thought about asking for a rain check as well, but she knew Kathleen; so she might as well get the interrogation over with. She knew Kathleen was going to get her when she found out she missed her date with Brian; but she would have to cut her some slack. After all, what choice did she have?

Kathleen stared at her in unbelief as she tried to understand exactly what Shirley was talking about. She let a total stranger move into her house; AND she missed her date with Brian! "What in the world were you thinking?

Did you at least call him Shirley?"

"Yes, I did. He wouldn't pick up his phone! Pass the jelly please," she asked hoping to lighten the mood, but it didn't help. The last thing she needed was a lecture about how she had failed her husband…again.

Sensing the tension in the air, Kathleen decided to take a more subtle approach on the subject of Nicole. "Nicole seems like a nice girl", she said.

Shirley looked at her, rolled her eyes and said, "Cut the crap, you already know you're dying to ask me why she is staying at my house. But that is the operative phrase, it's MY house, and I can have anyone I want at MY house." snapped Shirley.

After she said it, she immediately felt guilty and apologized. It wasn't Kathleen that she was irritated with, although her questions did get under her skin. This thing going on with Brian was the real issue, and it was driving her nuts. They were eating their food when this lady walks across the room and sat at their table. She looked a little familiar, although she could not really place the face.

"Hi, I'm Robin. I was wondering if you had seen Gwen lately." she said.

"No. Why would I have seen Gwen?" questioned Shirley a little confused.

"Well, I just thought you would have, being that she's doing your husband."

With that she got up and walked away from the table, leaving Shirley flabbergasted and irate. She felt the heat rush to her face, and she heard Kathleen calling her, "Shirley, are you okay?"

That hussy! She had the nerve to come and interrupt her breakfast and then walk away smiling like she had given her a bouquet of flowers. Is that why he had really moved out? Had he moved on with Gwen?

"Lord You gon' to have to help me. Don't let me act like I really want to. I am so angry. Please, Lord; help me before I go street up in here!" she prayed. She felt a little peace, but she was still mad. She warned him about that girl. She got up and asked the waiter for the check.
Kathleen almost laughed to keep from crying. What in the world was that woman thinking?! She's lucky she didn't get killed. She felt sorry for anyone who dared to cross Shirley. She didn't get mad often, but when she did, you could almost see the smoke blowing out of her ears. Boy, she thought to herself. She would hate to be Brian or Gwen, when Shirley caught up with them. She was a nice person, but when it came to Brian, she was like a lioness; definitely something to be feared.

Against Gwen's better judgment, she agreed to meet Robin at Omelet House for breakfast. Robin said it was imperative that she meet her right away. As she walked in, she saw Robin waving at her; and then she saw Shirley walking her way. She looked really angry. It didn't take too long for her to realize she had been set up. What in the world did she just walk into? "Whatever the enemy is planning for me, please turn it around and use it for Your glory," Gwen prayed. "And Lord, I can really use Your help!"

Shirley looked up and saw Gwen walk through the door. The nerve of this woman! She had the gall to flaunt her tail right in front of her. Lord, have mercy she was angry. The thought of this woman and Brian! He wouldn't have slept with another woman, would he? She thought she knew almost everything about him. Maybe she was mistaken. What in the world was going on?!

"Shirley!" Kathleen exclaimed.
But Shirley didn't want to talk to Kathleen. She wanted answers from this woman. The tramp who thought she

could just walk in and destroy her marriage. Before she knew it, she marched straight up to Gwen and asked her,

"Are you sleeping with my husband?"

"Shirley, I don't know what Robin told you, but we need to sit down and talk." said Gwendolyn.

"Talk? It seemed like a straightforward question to me. It's either yes or no." demanded Shirley.

"I would like to talk to you, just not here and not now. You need to calm down." Gwen said.

"No, she didn't just tell you to calm down, and she is having sex with your husband," Robin said, adding coal to the already burning fire.

Now every eye in the restaurant was on them. Gwen knew that somehow she needed to get Shirley to realize that this was not the time or the place.

"Lord, just in case you didn't hear me earlier when I prayed, now would be a good time for You to step in and say something! Hello, Lord, do You hear me?" she prayed silently.

Brian looked at the documents that his friend, who was now his lawyer, had drawn up for his divorce. If the divorce was uncontested, it could be final by the middle of next month. Fifteen years of marriage, and it's dissolved just like that; like it never existed. He wished getting over her was as easy as signing on a dotted line. She called this morning, but what was she going to give him another excuse as to why he was always the last one on her to do list? Well, he was sick and tired of all the little emergencies, and he was sick and tired of being in love with a woman who was "superhero" to the world.

When he told Mike to draw up the papers, he knew it was not God's will for him to leave Shirley. Somewhere deep inside, he knew he needed to stay with his wife, but he was tired of the struggle, and he was spent. Surely God could understand that he had given it all he could and he had nothing else left. Besides, God wasn't saying much to him at all, lately. It seemed like he couldn't get a break anywhere. The pastor kept calling him wanting to know where he had been. Come to think of it, he couldn't remember the last time he had been to church. What was the point in going? He felt alone and fallible. Where was God when he really needed Him? Yes, God was still on His throne, high and lifted up …. But, when it came to Brian (it seemed), He turned a deaf ear. Or was he too far away to hear Him?

"Shirley, I really can't do this with you right now. We can talk, just not now. I know you are angry, but let's discuss this in a right manner." and with that Gwen turned around and walk out of the restaurant. She was tempted to look over her shoulder, but she kept walking, got in her car and drove away. It wasn't until she was far away that she pulled over and took a deep breath and prayed. It seemed like that's all she did lately. She wasn't sure what to do, and she really needed God's guidance. It seemed like no matter how fast she ran; her past kept catching up to her. Her cell phone began ringing, and she unzipped her purse and answered it. "Hello, this is Gwen."

"Hi, Gwen! This is Linda. What's up? Do you have time to meet me for coffee? I have a proposition for you"

"Sure, I can use any type of distraction. I've had one heck of a day." Gwen stated wearily.

"Meet me at Starbucks right around the corner from your house, in twenty minutes."
Gwen looked around and realized that's where she had pulled over. She was sitting in the parking lot. Was it an appointment designed by God; or was it a mere coincidence that she just so happened to pull over in the same place Linda wanted to meet? Maybe God is present in things

than we think, she thought as she got out of her car and went in to reserve a table for them.

Shirley was flustered when she reached her car. She was infuriated by the thought that Brian had taken fifteen plus years of her life. If she counted the seven years they dated, then it was twenty-two years. She had given this man twenty-two years and he had the audacity to give himself to a woman like Gwen! Gwen of all women! If he was going to cheat, he could have at least done it with a woman of the same caliber as herself.

He had just thrown their marriage away. She didn't think she could ever forgive him. How could he do this to her? She was cool when he had said, "They needed a break," and she was even okay when he said he had "fallen out of love with her". She had even kept her cool when he had decided to move out. But dagnabit, he crossed the line! "Not today, partner!" she said as she made a U-turn in the middle of the street. She was going to his house, and she was getting some answers.

Kathleen was mumbling something about hearing his side before she over-reacted. What did she know? Danny worshipped the ground she walked on. So, even though she knew her friend was trying to help, right now she wished she would just shut up. The voice of reason was not what she wanted to hear right now. She wanted to be mad, and just for a moment, get even. She wanted him to feel the pain that was sinking deep into the pit of her stomach.

~

Brian heard tires screeching up to his drive way, and he heard a loud knock on the door. It was Shirley. He sat the papers on the counter and went to open the door. As he opened the door, she just barged in almost knocking him over. He was slightly taken aback for a minute. He locked the door and turned around to face her accusing eyes.

"What are you doing here?" asked Brian.

"I just ran into your little girlfriend! When were you going to tell me, Brian? "Look Shirley, I don't wanna get into all this. If you were so concerned about me, you wouldn't have had me sitting here last night waiting on you!" replied Brian.

"Well apparently, you weren't alone. When were you gonna tell me? I know you were sleeping with that tramp?" snorted Shirley.

He could see that she was not going to go away. "I don't know what you want me to say. Shirley? Gwen is not our problem. Our issues are between me and you." answered Brian.

"So you know who I'm talking about?" said Shirley.

Brian almost wanted to laugh. He had never seen her so mad. Although he wished it wasn't directed at him, this is the most emotion he had ever seen out of her. He needed to put some distance between them to give him time to think. "Dang! Gwen had gone to his wife?" he thought. She had unleashed a fury she wasn't able to handle. He wondered what the conversation ended like. Had she really told her they slept together? He thought something he said that night got through to her, but obviously he was wrong.

He proceeded to go into the kitchen and get a drink of water. Shirley stormed in right behind him. He sat his glass down; he noticed she had stopped talking. When he looked up at her she was staring at the divorce papers. "Shirley I'm sorry," he said, but he was too late. She slapped him so hard across his face that she had made him mad. He had never been so ready to knock a woman out as he was now.

"Whatcha gonna do, hit me?" she asked egging him on.

"No, but you better be on your way to wherever you're going. You better not slap me like that again! I can't promise you I'll be able to take it so nicely next time," he said as he glared at her. Sometimes, this woman made him so mad. She was the only one who really knew how to get under his skin, and right now she needed to get up out of his house.

Kathleen sat in the car wondering what in the world was going on. She knew they needed their privacy, but she also knew that Shirley was kinda crazy right now. Ultimately, she didn't know if there was really anything she could do. She heard a door slam, and out came Shirley. She was so mad, she was sweating. She threw open the car door, slammed it shut, and screeched back out of his driveway (almost hitting a car on the other side of the street). After a moment of strange silence, Kathleen said, "I just have one question. Is Brian still alive?"

Shirley started laughing so hard that she had to pull over. "Have I gone that insane that you thought I might kill him?" She was laughing so hard that tears began to flow from her eyes. "Kat, he had divorce papers drawn up," she said between her laughter and tears. Soon the laughter left, and the tears continued flowing.

"Are you okay? I know all this must be difficult to deal with." Kathleen said at last.

"I'll be alright. It just seems so unfair. I'm really angry he didn't even bother trying to explain," Shirley cried.

"So you think he really did have an affair with Gwen?"

"I didn't even have to say who I was talking about. He already knew it was Gwen."

"Shirley, that doesn't prove anything."

"What! Are you suddenly in his amen corner, Kat?"

"No! I just know you guys have something special. I would hate to see you throw your marriage down the drain based on an assumption, especially since both of you are too stubborn to find out the truth," reasoned Kathleen.

This had gone on long enough; she was going to talk some sense into Shirley whether she liked it or not. Keep me, Lord Jesus!

Gwen sat at the table, waiting for Linda to come in. She decided to order a chocolate chip banana muffin as she waited. She was enjoying her muffin so much that she didn't notice Linda come in.

"You haven't eaten today, I see," said Linda jokingly.

"No, I really haven't eaten. Sit down. I'm having a dolce latté with caramel sauce. What kind of coffee do you want?" Gwen asked.

"I'll have the same. Just make mine a sugar free one. I've got to get ready for my wedding!" Linda exclaimed.

"What! Girl, are you kidding?" asked Gwen.

"Nope, he asked me last night!" Linda was beaming.

"Wow! That is wonderful," she said with all the emotion she could muster up. Although she was happy for her, she was sure this was the end of their friendship.

"What's the matter?" asked Linda quizzically, seeing the look on Gwen's face.

"Did you bring me here to tell me we can't be friends anymore? I don't have a good reputation with married women. Heck, I don't have a good reputation with most women. It seems like every time I turn around, I'm the one getting left."

"Umm... I don't have a clue what you are talking about! We're stuck for life, sister! You couldn't get rid of me if you tried! God made you my new sister, and that comes with the good, the bad, and the ugly. You need to quit replaying the past and make some new memories. People see you how you see yourself. Stop putting an old label on your new self. Yes, you have made mistakes, but the mistakes made you who you are today. Don't run away from them or allow yourself to be shamed by them. I want you to remember this: The past does not dictate your position in Christ. Girl, you better get out of that pity party! I'm not going there with you. You better start learning to talk back to that devil and let him know that you can't be punked into any title he just decides to slap on you. You better stop answering to those names and start walking in the victory of Christ. And that's all I have to say about that!" concluded Linda with a smirk.

It seemed that no matter how fast she ran, she couldn't get away from who she was. Gwen finally understood; the answer was not to run away from the past, but to learn from it and allow God to use it to deliver others. For the first time, she did not feel ashamed. It was as if a light bulb flashed on her brain. Jesus paid the price, and it was up to her to walk in the victory.

"Look, Kathleen, it's not like this situation is your area of expertise. This is not some book you're writing. It's your life! If Danny cheated on you, would we still be having this conversation?" After a long pause, she looked up and saw the sadness in Kathleen's eyes, and she realized she had stuck her foot in her mouth one more time.

"Yes, Shirley, we would. He had an affair after three years of marriage." As she told Shirley the story, she realized this was the last secret she kept from her best friend. She still remembered it just like it was yesterday.

Danny called her at work and said he needed to talk to her. So, Kathleen left work early. She walked in to their house and past his suitcases packed by the front door. She sat down next to him, and he began to tell her the story. Danny desperately wanted a baby, and she couldn't give him one. For some reason her body rejected the embryo and expelled it soon after it implanted.

Danny always wanted to talk about what it would be like with his son or daughter, but she wanted him to just be happy with her. What if she could never give him a baby? The wall between them grew bigger and bigger. Kathleen didn't want to talk to Danny anymore about having a family, so she stopped talking all together. He wanted to have sex as often as they could because he heard it could help the odds of the pregnancy. He even bought fertility books and printed articles on specialists in the area. It was too much pressure for Kathleen. She desired sex less and less, and pretty soon she just did it out of obligation.

Danny began to question her incessantly, and this led to arguments - many, many arguments. She knew if they argued he would leave her alone, and it worked. He eventually moved out of their room and into the room they hoped would become the baby's nursery one day. Kathleen turned to writing, and Danny had turned to a friend. At first, she seemed to be a listening ear, but a bond developed over time. Six months later he was telling her that all the business trips he had supposedly taken, he actually spent with a girl named Erica. Danny realized he was wrong and ended things, but he didn't want to live a lie anymore. He said he was sorry, and he wanted to be with her, but if she wanted him to leave he would understand.

She remembered how his betrayal devastated her. She told him he could still stay in the house, but she wasn't sure if she would ever let him back into her heart. Months passed, and she felt like she was ready to try to put the affair behind them. They went to counseling and met other couples who lived through affairs. One day after a group session, she asked him why he wanted to stay married to her. He told her that his life would be empty without her, and he was sure that God could resurrect their marriage. He believed that she was his "virtuous woman" and he was her "man of valor". It took them a while to move past it, but she had stayed and fought for their marriage.

"Danny was a good man. He just got caught up in something he had no business being in," Kathleen said. "Don't let one stupid mistake ruin your future together. God did it for us, and we had nine happy years together after the affair. Life is too short. Tomorrow is not promised." Shirley needed to understand that while there are numerous counterfeit relationships, she and Brian's was the real thing. They couldn't just give up! "I know you don't want to hear this, but I'm going to say it anyway. You need to stop focusing on everyone else and pay some attention to your husband."

"So, you're saying it's my fault he cheated on me?" asked Shirley angrily.

"No, that is not what I am saying. I'm saying that your life is built around everyone else's emergencies. I'm saying... everything takes a back seat to the emergency of the day. Not that you are wrong for helping people, but you have to take care of home first. It's time for you to take some of your own advice girl, and fix your marriage. Fight for him, let him know you love him, and let God restore your marriage. Its tight, but you know it is right."
It was so quiet in the car; you could almost hear a pin drop.

"It's too late I already signed the papers!" Shirley said quietly as she maneuvered the steering wheel and pulled back into traffic heading back home.

Brian sat there and stared at his divorce papers. He sighed, but the much-needed breath did not remove the knot in his throat. He expected her to make a small protest, but she hadn't. Shirley just signed the papers, slammed them down on the counter, and ran out of the house like a maniac. His marriage had been reduced to a couple of signatures. It was over. Why did his gut tell him to run out after Shirley and tell her all this had been a misunderstanding, to beg her to take him back? Brian knew she would never take him back. Nope. Not now. Not when she felt betrayed. She would never forgive him.

Maybe God was wrong. Maybe some things couldn't be resurrected. Well, it was over now. He would just move on with his life, but somehow he knew that his life would never be the same from this moment on.

Nobody said a word as Kathleen and Shirley pulled into the driveway. It was Kathleen who finally broke the silence. "Shirley, you and Brian love each other, and you guys can work through this. I don't care if you have signed the papers. You need to fight for this marriage."

"What do you want me to say, that I still love him? Yes, I still love him! The bottom line is, while he was telling me he missed me, he was having an affair with another woman and for that, I hate him! He walked out on me! Remember that? I'm tired of being the one trying to hold on to someone who doesn't give a hoot about me. If he did, he never would have left."

"You don't even know if there was an actual affair. Brian left because he panicked, and that's what people do after a tragedy, Shirley! It's easier to run than to deal with the problem. Please don't run, Shirley," Kathleen pleaded. "You guys have too much together to let anything come between you two."

"No, Kat. I'm not the one that let anything come between us, he did. I just don't have the energy to fight anymore."

"What about God? You're telling me it's too much for you, but is it too much for God? It's time to put your faith where your mouth is. Stop giving up, and start getting mad. You are allowing the enemy to come in and devour your home. Aren't you the one who is always telling me we wrestle not against flesh and blood? Faith isn't needed when you can see an expected end, Shirley!" Kathleen said it with so much passion she surprised herself.

Shirley wanted to be mad, but she knew Kat was right. God made her a promise and how quickly she had forgotten the very words He spoke to her heart. She felt her eyes welling up with tears. Her life, as she knew it, was falling apart; and who was this stranger sitting in the car with her? When did she get so smart?

~

Gwen looked at the designs she had sketched; they were okay, but she was not impressed. Linda asked her to design her wedding. This was something she really enjoyed doing and, oh man, this was a big project -- big enough to keep her busy for a while. They were planning on getting married on New Year's Eve. Linda kept after her about her starting her own business, and she thought this just might be it. Decorating homes and businesses was okay, but they were nowhere near as thrilling as putting on a once in a lifetime storybook wedding. Something seemed to be missing, and then it dawned on her. Cinderella was too played out. She could do a "jazz under the stars" theme. It would be perfect! She pulled out fresh paper to begin her sketch. Now, with a new inspiration, her creative juices began to flow. She was sure Linda was thrilled .

Chamber four

The last few weeks had been an adjustment for Shirley. The finality of her marriage was terrifying for her, but she had decided to get her head in the game and test the waters. Brian wasn't the only one capable of moving on.
She had met a man named Greg. They had been talking a couple of weeks, and when they found out they lived in the same city, they decided to meet. Kathleen had nearly blown a gasket when she had found out Shirley had agreed to meet him today.

"You are supposed to be the sensible one." You don't know anything about him. He could be a serial killer or a rapist! What if he is married with six kids?" she said, "You guys would always be broke by the time he finished paying child support. Besides, you are still married, Shirley. How can you even contemplate dating somebody else?" she pouted.

"Kathleen, slow down. I'm just meeting him, and the last time I checked, I was grown and I didn't need to run my decisions by anyone!" said Shirley. Why did it seem like everyone kept forgetting that Brian was the one who decided he wanted out? She had just given him what he had wished for. What was she supposed to do, curl up and die? She was not about to give him his cake and his ice cream, too, while she waited at home for him to come to his senses and choose her. No way! She was not the one. And, besides, Greg seemed harmless enough. She had nothing to feel guilty about! Did she? It was just lunch and at Chicago Joe's. If this date did turned out to be a bust, at least her taste buds would not be disappointed.

She arrived at the restaurant early and took a table nestled in a cozy corner. Chicago Joe's was not only well known for their food but also for their relaxing ambiance. Although the mood had been set, she was having a hard time relaxing; she found herself fidgeting as she waited for him. She had agreed to wear a yellow rose in her hair, so that he would know who she was. But she could not help feeling like she was overdressed; maybe she should have elected to wear jeans instead of the chic red dress she had on. Now, she was wishing she hadn't gone for the classy, sexy look and had opted for the relaxed yet sophisticated look.

Oh well, it's done now, she sighed. She didn't know what he looked like although she wasn't caught up totally on looks. She was not about to waste her time with any broke down-looking man. She saw several men walk in, but not one had approached her. Then from across the room, she spotted this gorgeous man; he was perfect. He was just the right color, not too dark but not too light. He had an athletic build, and he was about 6'2" tall. His features were almost too perfect to be a man, and as he walked to the table, she couldn't help but smile when he introduced himself as Greg.

She quickly forgot her nervousness as she focused her attention on her date. "Have you lived in Vegas all your life?" she asked Greg. "Yeah, sort of, how about you?" he answered.

"Yes, pretty much. I was born in California, but my family moved here when I was eight months old, and I have been here since. To tell you the truth, I can't imagine living anywhere else."

"What do you do for a living?" she asked him. "I am sort of in the ministry." he answered. He was kind of vague with his answers, but just as she was about to ask him why, the waiter came and soon she had forgotten her questions about his vagueness when she found herself knee deep in delectable entrees, wading through to a decision. She decided finally after a lot of thought to have the Seafood

Alfredo platter with chunks of mouthwatering lobster and crab adorned with colossal shrimp and drizzled with a creamy garlic Alfredo sauce beautifully arranged on a bed of linguini. Greg decided on the spaghetti. She could tell by his choice in entrées that he liked to play it safe. He was a cautious man.

For the first time, she realized this was her first real date; her only interactions with a man had been with Brian. Nervousness began to set in; maybe Kathleen was right, maybe she was in over her head. They proceeded with the normal small talk on a first date, but things began to heat up when he said,

"Have you even been in love?" She stammered over her answer. "Yes, I don't know, maybe so; I mean, I thought I was. My first love has been my husband for the last fifteen years, and then out of the blue he moves out, and now we are in the process of a divorce." she said hesitatingly. "How about you?" she asked. So much for small talk, she thought.

"I know love, and I know that there is no emotion that is greater than love. It's forgiving, it's patient, and it's nurturing; it's almost as if people lose all ability to reason when they are in love. It's wonderful and a true gift when it is experienced in the true form it was created for. " he said. "Why do you think that so many people search for true love, but so many people never find it?" he asked. "What do you mean? she asked. There are a lot of people in love.". "I didn't say in love, I said true love." he answered. "What's the difference?" she asked. "It's really just a play on words."

"There is a big difference. When I look around I see so many counterfeit copies of people willing to settle because, in truth, they don't think that they deserve any more. God created love and everything about it is wonderful. Being vulnerable to someone and sharing the most intimate parts of your life with that person; there is nothing more precious than true love." he answered.

"Yeah" she said as she smirked. "You just need to make sure you give yourself to the right person. If not, you will end up like me, giving yourself and still being left behind." She wasn't sure if she would ever be able to let her guard down and give herself to someone completely. Did she really want to? After all, she had given herself completely and where had it gotten her? Starting over again at thirty-four, when she had planned to have everything in order by now; and she could not believe she was starting all over again.

"Let me ask you a question and if it is too personal, I'll understand. He paused a moment and then asked,

"Why are you getting divorced?"

She was a little surprised by the bluntness of his question. She was tempted to tell him it was none of his business, but then she saw something in his eyes that made her feel comfortable. It was like she had known him forever. He was looking at her so intently; it was like his dark brown eyes twinkled as they searched her eyes for clues into her soul.

"I don't know. We started out pretty good but then something changed along the way. Then we took a break, and the next thing I know, we are getting divorced. In addition, he is having an affair. That about sums it up," she said, "the story of my life."

Greg paused for a minute, and then he said "Have you told him you don't want a divorce?" "I mean you still are very much in love with him." he finished.

"I'm not in love with him anymore," she said quickly, even though she knew when she uttered the words, that her statement was not true. She really wanted to believe that she could just move on. But somehow she wondered could she ever untangle her heart from being intertwined with his when it needed his to somehow navigate through this dimension she called life?

She took a deep breath and then said, "Enough about me and Brian, already" as she poured a glass of champagne. "To new beginnings," she said as she handed him a glass. Shirley lifted her glass for a toast.

The clinking of the glass to her symbolized shedding of the old and moving on into the new. She gazed at him shyly; this Greg was an odd fellow, like no one she had ever met. She knew so little about him, yet she was drawn to know more. She took a small sip of champagne, and thought it odd when he sat his glass back on the table untouched; she shrugged, thinking he must not be a champagne type of man.

He just sat with eyes focused directly on her, not saying a word just staring at her like he could look right through her. After what seemed like an eternity, he finally spoke:

"Shirley, I know that you are hurting, but your marriage still has some hope; things are not what they appear to be. Find it in your heart to forgive, and God will do the rest."

"Um, Greg, did you hear me say that he had an affair?

He broke our wedding vows. And I'm supposed to just get over it, right? And play the doting wife?" said Shirley as she scanned the room looking for the waiter, hoping he would soon bring their food. Maybe an interruption would help shift the focus off of her.

"So, being here with me is to get back at him for being unfaithful to you? But really you don't care about him; that's why you are sitting here with me -- because you don't have anything to prove to him. Did I get it right?" chuckled Greg.

Boy, he had some nerve, making fun at her. She did not find his joke at all amusing, considering her emotions were the butte of his comedy routine. She had had more than enough of Dr. Phil with all his answers and the "How's it working for you" mentality. "My marriage lost its hope the day my husband decided to let a tramp replace his wife." she said angrily.

"No, your marriage died the day you decided to stop fighting. The day you lost the vision that God placed in your heart." he said. He spoke with so much confidence she had to admit she questioned for a moment how he seemed to know so much about her and Brian.

"How do you know anything about my marriage? How dare you sit there hurling accusations about me as if you have any right to judge me? I don't have anything left to give. My marriage is dead, over and done. So is this date!" she said. She was getting out of here; she was not about to sit here. Who the heck did he think he was, patronizing her? She was so beyond finished listening to him talk about her life like he even had a clue about her life. She tried to gather her composure and got up from the table, knocking down her drink right in her lap. The champagne was so cold as it trickled down her leg. "So much for my new beginning!" she thought as she scurried to her feet, bumping the waiter and knocking a plate of spaghetti right on Greg's pants. "I'm so sorry," she stammered, knocking over his glass in the process of reaching for a napkin...right on the front of his perfectly pressed white shirt. It was something like in a movie, but sadly, it was seemingly an indicator of all the botched up messes in her life. Why was she so good at organizing other people's lives, but when it came to her, she ran out of answers? She stared at Greg, horrified about what he must be thinking instead of him being a psycho. Somebody should have warned Greg about the crazy date he would meet on the internet.

Then he started laughing. He had a beautiful baritone

laugh, which began to cut through the tension surrounding them in the room. They stared at each other and then they started laughing so hard that everyone began to turn around and stare at them, but she just couldn't help it; it had been so long since she had laughed, really laughed, and it felt so good. She felt a release in her spirit, and the weight that had bogged down her petite frame temporarily fled.

"Talk about shooting the messenger," he said as he scooped the soggy meatballs and sauce from his pants and attempted to pat the huge stain on the front of his shirt.

"You know, you could have just said, 'I don't want to answer." he said between chuckles.

"Me and Brian used to be so happy." she said. "We used to laugh so hard. And we would talk for so many hours about nothing. Greg I don't know what happened. I know he wants a baby so bad, and I don't know if I will ever be able to give him one. What if me allowing him to go, allows him to have the deepest desire of his heart and what if deep down inside I am afraid that I am not enough?" she said. "What if letting him go is easier than facing my inability as a woman to reproduce?"

Her laughter had long since fled and was soon replaced with sobs. Her heart was breaking and it hurt…it hurt so badly. She stood blindly in the middle of the restaurant, crying. She could not believe she was having a total meltdown in the front of a total stranger and room full of people. She felt like she was going to have a panic attack as her eyes bulged from her struggling to breathe. Her heart pounded so hard that she could hear it pulsating in her temples.

Almost instinctively Greg quickly got up, handed her a napkin, put his arm protectively around her shoulders and guided her toward the door of the restaurant into the fresh air. The fresh air tasted so good even though she was sure it was laced with smog from the overpopulated city. He guided her through the parking lot and to his car. After making sure she was safely in he told her he needed to go back in to settle the check, and then he would be back. He came back carrying their dinner in foil containers.

"Oh my God, he probably thinks I'm crazy!" she said as she sat there horrified but still unable to stop the flow of tears. The waves of emotions that hit her body were unbelievable. Why had she let herself be so vulnerable to a total stranger? And now he probably thought she was a maniac, maybe a bit psychopathic. There was probably not probability of another date. She blew it, and they hadn't even gotten through lunch. And the worst part was she was still hungry.

He started the car and headed toward her house; they were both quiet. Shirley was so embarrassed; she didn't know what to say. They coasted up to her driveway, and it was Greg who finally broke the silence

"Shirley, I need to tell you something; you and Brian have something special, and God wants you to know that He hears you."

"He loves you. Let him take your pain and He will restore your life and everything that has been taken from you. Forgive Brian quickly; you don't know how short life is. Make the most of your life while you have a chance. Tomorrow is not promised to anyone. Don't let pride and unforgiveness plague your life; you have a wonderful heart and you are full of love." He pleaded for her to understand. She stood there, staring at him and wondering why the only man she had picked to go on a date would be the man to plead Brian's case before her. "Just my luck!" she said to herself. "Greg, you don't understand. I can't forgive him. I won't allow him to make me into his fool. He left me. He made his choice." she said.

Tears in the Chambers of Heaven

"No, you made the choice to let him go. And if you didn't still love him, why are you so emotional at the thought of moving on?" he said gently.

"What in the world? He had an affair, moved out on me and filed for a divorce, and you say I let him go? No. He wanted to go! He packed his suitcase and rented an apartment. If that wasn't enough, Mr. Advocate of Brian, he hired his girlfriend to decorate his apartment. Maybe you should know the story before you offer your little two cents."

"Hold on, slow down," he said with a smile. "You have a lot of wisdom when it comes to other people, but you, my dear, are going to lose everything if you don't wake up and take control of your life!" said Greg. "Really, Brian is not the cause of your unhappiness." You are! And your inability to forgive." he said. "When are you going to truly allow yourself to admit that you need somebody and you don't have all the answers?"

"God is waiting on you to surrender everything to him, and you will get the desires of your heart" he concluded. "What do you know about me?" she asked angrily. She could not believe that she was getting so mad, but who was he to tell her that she was playing a victim. In most cases she would have excused herself from his car and chalked it up to a bad date, but somehow she just couldn't, so she sat listening to the man talk to her like he knew her and, in truth, they really had just met.

After a brief silence, Greg said, "I know more than you think I do, I know that you throw yourself into helping others because something deep inside says that if you help them straighten out their lives, you won't need to admit that you need help with your life." "I know that God loves you; that's why he sent me to help you from messing up one of the best gifts he ever gave you." said Greg. "He won't force you to stay. But if you continue with this divorce, you will be outside of the will of God.

"Well, tell me this -- will you ask God a question for me? Since you seem to be in tight with Him. If it is out of God's will to get this divorce, then why did He let Brian file for it? And tell me, why did He allow Gwendolyn to seduce my husband? If it's supposed to be my gift, why is she the one who is enjoying it?" she snapped. Greg stood there looking at Shirley. Standing before him was a wounded little girl, taking blind swings with her eyes closed and hoping to make contact with her unseen enemy.

She was unmistakably beautiful; her delicate skin, her almond-shaped eyes, even the way her mouth curled and the vein popped out in her temple when she was mad. She had no clue the destiny that she would soon walk into if she could just get past all the pain and allow God to help her.

Greg touched her shoulder, gently lifted her head so that her eyes met his, and said, "Beloved, why won't you hold on to the promise that God is in control and stand firm on what God has said? He loves you, and you bring him so much joy. He listens for you, Shirley; where have you been? He misses you.

She could see that the words were spoken with so much tenderness that it sent chills through her body; it felt like a wet blanket had been placed on her shoulders. Why was this man saying all these things? Why couldn't he leave well enough alone? This date had not gone at all how she had planned. She had hoped to have forgotten all about Brian by now, and here she was, more frustrated and confused than when the date had first begun.

"You never lost your joy. The real reason you don't have emotions is because you never let anyone close enough to you. People are closer to you than you are to them. Share your life, let someone in. That is why God made you relational, but I'll tell you this; it's going to be a lonely road with no one to share. He concluded: "It's a gift, but a gift needs to be received and given in order to accomplish its purpose." What was he talking about and why was everything about him a riddle? Why did she feel like he knew so much about her and her life but he still seemed to remain a mystery?

She didn't know what to say. Part of her wanted to stay angry at Greg, but the other part felt comforted by the authority that he spoke with.

"I know you think that you know me." Shirley said with a small pause. "Greg, maybe not every marriage is made to stand the test of time."

"Are you sure that this is a marriage ordained by God, Shirley?" he asked.

"I was at one time, but honestly now I don't know. It's falling apart, and there is nothing I can do to stop it.," she said. "So, what made you think your marriage was ordained by God in the beginning?" asked Greg. "Because I was so sure that I heard God; it may sound silly, but I was sure God spoke to me." she said. "So, did God change, or did you change? Because God's word cannot return void." Greg said.

"I do love my husband, but he made his choice, and I can't make someone stay with me if they want to leave. What am I supposed to do? Beg him to stay, even though he wants to leave?" She blinked hard, trying to keep the tears from escaping her eyes. She had already made a fool of herself, and she was determined to gain control over her emotions.

"No, you need to forgive Brian and let God worry about the rest! He is fully capable, but the wonderful part is that He is willing! Shirley, it's been wonderful meeting you and I know that you and Brian will be okay. Just trust God.

"Yeah, it's been interesting to say the least." said Shirley. "Don't call me, I'll call you," Shirley said to herself. Although Greg seemed to be a nice man, he definitely wouldn't be getting another call from her although she had to admit he did leave her with a lot to think about. He hugged her goodbye. "Have a good night. I know that you are angry with me, but you'll soon see I am right." He kissed her on her forehead, walked her up to the door and then left.

She stood on her porch for a long time, looking up at the sky, amazed by the vastness of God's creativity. Sometimes He felt so far away, but sometimes He felt so close that she could reach out and grab His hand.   "Lord, I have really made a mess of things. I don't know where to start. I'm scared I am going to lose him, but I'm scared I don't have the energy to fight to keep him. Lord, please tell me what I'm supposed to do."

"What do you want?" said a small whisper, almost as if passing in the wind. The voice was unmistakable; it was God. It had been a long time since she had heard Him. She used to remember the times as a young girl when she would hear Him call her name, and instantly she would know who He was. Sometimes, it would be an audible voice, but sometimes it would be a word spoken to her heart. She couldn't explain the joy that filled her heart as she heard Him. She had called and He had come. "What do you want?" said the voice, this time a little louder.

"I want to let go; it's too heavy for me to carry." She felt like a little child who had fallen and run to its mother for comforting. She felt beat up… used up… and fed up. This time, she was alone, and she didn't feel like she needed to keep up appearances.

She let go of the last rein she was holding, "Lord, I need to trust You completely."

"Will You help me trust You completely with my life?" she asked.

"Do you love me, Shirley?" he said. "Yes, Lord" she said. "Is there anything too big for me to do?" He asked. "No Lord, you can do anything you want to do." she answered. "Then stand still, and see that I am God!"

And she felt peace begin to chip away the clouds of gloom that had somehow seeped into her spirit, casting doubt. She knew God was in control, and as long as He was in control, she could have peace. Soon, the sun began to set; it was so beautiful, she wondered how many times she had seen the sunset. And yet, she was amazed every time she saw it, and it always seemed that every sunset was even more beautiful than the last. She just wanted to stay outside and bask underneath the night sky in the presence of God. She stood there dumbfounded; she felt so tiny underneath the blanket of stars. It seemed like hours before she could finally tear herself away, promising herself to spend more time listening for God's voice. Her life always seemed so chaotic, but she needed to spend some time in the presence of God. Her soul longed for that connection. She had somehow forgotten the joy of loving God.

She went inside the house and laid her keys on the counter. She had to admit, though, her spirit was revived; her body just had to take a bath and go to bed.

She saw the answering machine message light blinking; she pushed the button. She had a message from Kathleen and some telemarketers and a brief message from her sister telling her it was important that she called her back. What in the world could she want?! She hadn't heard from her sister in so long. Not since the death of their dad. Although she was curious, her sister would have to wait. She didn't have enough energy to deal with her tonight. The last message was from an unfamiliar voice. She played the message through a second time because he was talking way too fast for her to understand. It was Greg, saying that he was not going to make it to their date because he had a family emergency. His voice didn't sound the same, and what was he talking about? He had dropped her off about an hour ago. He left a number. She picked up the phone and dialed the number, and he picked up the phone.

"Hello," she said, "I think I misunderstood your message." she said. "You said you had a family emergency?" "Yes, I am so sorry, baby" he said, "My son fell and broke his leg and that stupid ex-wife of mine wanted me to be at the hospital with him. So, when can we hook up?" he asked. "Hook up" -- what in the world was he taking about? Was he crazy, or was she finally losing it? "I'm not sure that is a good idea," she said. "Oh, come on, sweetheart, you know I would have been there with you instead of some dumb hospital." He mumbled some obscene words to some kids in the background. She was deeply repulsed by him and his language. "I think we need to quit while we are ahead," she said, not sure what was going on or why she felt like somehow she had been propelled into the twilight zone. "What? I thought we had made a connection." "Why you suddenly doggin' me" he said. "Look, Greg, what you are saying is that you never showed up to the restaurant?" "I just told you that while I was leaving to come, my ex-wife called me, and I spent the rest of the evening at the hospital." he said, irritated "Tell me, what did you wear? No, better yet, tell me what you have on now." he said. "At least this whole night doesn't have to be a total dud." he said, trying to make his voice deep and sexy. He made her want to vomit. "Look, Greg, please don't call me again; it's been a thrill," she said sarcastically "but you're really not my type." He mumbled something inaudible and hung up the phone. She stood there for a long time with the dial tone blaring in her ear. She felt the warm blanket around her shoulders as she stood there, trying to grasp what had just happened. What in the world was he talking about? Then, suddenly she felt the chills racing through her body, and she knew! She wasn't for sure, but she thought she may have just encountered an angel at the restaurant. Then she began to fit the pieces together, like how he seemed to know so much about her, and then she remembered she hadn't even told him where she lived. They had driven separate vehicles to the restaurant. Oh, no! And her car was still at the restaurant. He also had a very calming effect even though he said some very confrontational stuff.

Wow! Could he had really have been an angel? His answers to most of her questions were vague. Shirley realized that God had already answered the questions she had just barley uttered on the porch. She was overwhelmed. The creator of the universe cared enough about her to answer her prayer before she could even pray it. That's the kind of God she served, the God that might not come when you want Him, but is always right on time.

~

Kathleen saw Gwendolyn sitting at the desk in her office on the telephone as she entered the building. She also noticed the surprised yet worried look on Gwendolyn's face when she looked up and saw her coming. Kathleen smiled, hoping to reassure her that she wasn't here to cause trouble.

"Hi, Gwendolyn, I need to talk to you." said Kathleen casually. Gwendolyn reluctantly met her gaze and said, "Let me tie up this call, and I will be right with you." She asked her to wait in the conference room next to her office.

Kathleen looked around the room as she waited. It was nicely decorated with bright colors, colors she would have never had chosen, but they looked wonderful together. She had to admit that although Gwendolyn was a tramp, she was talented.

After a short time, Gwen came in carrying two bottles of water and a Coke and said nervously, "I thought you might like something to drink." "Sure, I'll take the water: I'm trying to eat healthy lately." Kathleen said as she pointed to her protruding belly, her stomach that was stretched as much as humanly possible, and to think she still had eleven weeks left. She flopped down in the chair at the conference table facing Gwen and said, "I guess you know why I'm here. I want the truth about you and Brian." Gwen took a swallow of her drink and then said, "I'm a little confused as to why you are here instead of Shirley? "I don't have anything to hide, but I just assumed that I would be having this conversation with her sooner or later." She finished and paused, waiting for an answer. "Well, she's not here; I'm here, and I want to know, are you sleeping with my best friend's husband?" Kathleen said as she stared at her, daring her to tell her a lie. Gwen shifted uncomfortably in her chair as she tried to avoid her stare.

"No, I'm not sleeping with him." she answered. "I knew it! Brian would never cheat on Shirley with you!" Kathleen said loudly, and then apologized.

"I'm sorry. I didn't mean it like that." said Kathleen. "No, really that's okay; I know exactly what you meant" said Gwendolyn.

At one time, I did try to sleep with him, but he couldn't because he loved Shirley, and I'm glad God kept us from making a bad decision. You have to believe me, I am not the same person I was then; I have really changed!" she said. Kathleen sized her up. She didn't look any different to her. She looked like the same tramp that had stolen other people's husbands in the past.

"Well, I just want you to know if you do have any plans for Brian, you need to forget them." Kathleen said accusingly. Now that she had the answer she wanted, she felt no need to sugar coat her response. The sight of this woman made her sick. How many homes had she broken up? Gwendolyn tried to hide the hurt look in her eyes as she shifted again in her chair. "Why are you looking so surprised, Gwen? When you have a reputation like yours, you have to have tough skin, right? You need to keep your little grubby hands off of my friend's husband because he will never be with someone who is the likes of you." said Kathleen. Gwen wanted to wipe that little smug look off her face, but she realized this was her opportunity to pass the test. She could finally conquer her shame.

"Look, Kathleen, I deserve much better than someone else's hand-me-downs. I don't want Brian or anyone else's man, for that matter. My only plans are to find what God has for me. I don't want the counterfeit copy. I want the real thing. And, you know what? I deserve it! If there is nothing else, you can see yourself out." she said to Kathleen. And with that, she excused herself, leaving Kathleen sitting there speechless.

For the first time in her life, Gwendolyn felt good; she knew who she was, and it didn't matter if Kathleen or anybody else believed she had changed. She didn't need their approval to validate herself. And she had to admit it felt good to realize God's love for her was not dependent on everyone else's opinion of her.

Brian surveyed the room. He still had so much to do; he hadn't realized that he had accumulated so much stuff in such a short amount of time. He had decided he needed a change in scenery. He had a friend in Portland who had been trying to get him for the longest time to come and help him with his law practice. And he had reluctantly agreed after realizing he needed to get as far away from Shirley as possible. Staying in the same town with Shirley was unbearable. He was never going to be completely rid of her until he moved on with his life. So, he figured he would take Mark up on his offer, and he had received his letter last week saying that he had been cleared to practice law in Oregon. So, he was packing up and moving on. He didn't see any reason for dragging his move out.

He had four days to pack up the apartment, and he was only taking the necessities right now. For the remainder, he was going to rent a storage room and leave it here for the time being. His ticket was for Friday at 6:00 a.m. And he would start work on Monday.

He looked at his watch and went to get the phone book because the movers were over an hour late. Just as he went to dial the number, he heard somebody ring the doorbell. He opened the door and there, standing in the doorway, was a man who was probably about thirty-four or thirty-five, with a big cheesy grin on his face. "Man, where y'all been?" he said. "And where are the rest of the movers?" Although Brian didn't have a lot of stuff, it was going to take more than one person to empty the place. "They will be here in a little bit." the man said. "Hello, my name is Max." he said, extending his hand. "It's my grandfather's company; I just help out here and there, and, as for your question about the movers, they should be on their way. I was supposed to meet them here."

"Hi, Max." said Brian, gripping his hand in a hand shake, "Come on in." He gestured him to go into the living room. "Wow," said Max as he looked at the pictures on the wall. "These are good. Did you take these pictures?"

"Yeah, it used to be something I really enjoyed doing." said Brian. "Wow, you are really talented; these pictures look so real. Well, I know they are of real people, but I mean that they really pull you into the moment, and you could almost feel their emotions." said Max, struggling to find the right words to give the pictures justification. And when he could find none, he just sighed at all these people, young and old, and all had a different key to the mystery of life. Every face represented a story and Brian had captured it in their eyes. "So, where are you moving?" asked Max.

"I'm moving to Portland; I am spreading my wings and flying."

"That is quite a contrast in climate and life style." he said. "I just need a change." Brian said. "How does your wife feel about the move?" asked Max. "How do you know I have a wife?" questioned Brian. Max pointed to Brian's wedding ring. "Oh, I forgot to take it off. Soon it will be official; we will be legally divorced. That's why I need a change; I am leaving a few days after court. The judge wants to meet us so that we can split up our assets." Max said, "I'm sorry, man. If you don't mind, can I ask you what happened?" "Well, life happened; one day we were happy, expecting our baby girl and then it was over, just like that and things haven't been the same since Destiny died. It was almost like we lost a connection somewhere." Brian had not allowed himself to think about Destiny in a long time. She thought I wanted a baby so bad, but in reality, all I have ever wanted is just her. I needed her, but she was always off somewhere else," he said. "Man, Brian, there has got to be something you can do! Do you still love her?" Max was puzzled; this man obviously still cared for his wife. And if indeed he did, why was he walking away? "Of course, I love her but it's too late. She doesn't love me anymore. You should have seen her face when she saw those divorce papers. No, she doesn't want anything else to do with me." he said.

"Look, have you told her you don't want a divorce?" Max asked. "Are you married?" asked Brian. "No, not me. I haven't even been close." said Max quickly. He wasn't against the thought of marriage, but he had never found the right one, and he had enough sense to wait until she came along. "One thing you have to learn about a woman -- once she's hurt, nothing you can say will change that until she wants to let you in again." said Brian "and right now, brother, she is finished with me." Max's cell phone began to ring. "Excuse me one moment." he said. It's my grandfather. "Hello" he said as Brian went into the kitchen to get some lemonade; it was a hot day, and he was sure that Max could use something to wet his throat. And, to tell the truth, Brian could use a distraction. Talking about Shirley had left a bitter taste in his mouth. They had been so happy at one time. What happened? They were a church-going couple and had devoted their lives to Christ. Shouldn't they have been immune to divorce? Now Brian didn't even want to go to church for fear that everyone knew what a failure he was.

"Hey, Brian that was my grandfather; he said it's taking them a little longer than they thought, and they will be here as soon as they can. Do you mind if I hang out until they get here?" he asked. "No, I don't mind; it is nice to have company even if you are nosey." said Brian playfully.

"Yeah, I've been told I have that problem," laughed Max.

"Hey, I know you are busy, but I would like to invite you to come to church next week, no pressure. It's just, I will be speaking, and this is my very first conference." said Max. "You didn't tell me you were a pastor." said Brian. "Well, not officially, my grandfather is the senior pastor, and I am just the associate pastor, but I have been invited to speak at a men's conference, and I would like you to come as one of my invited guests." he said. "Well, I haven't exactly been in the church all too much lately," said Brian sheepishly. "Man, don't go getting all weird on me because you find out I'm a preacher." he said disappointedly. It seemed like every time he made a connection with people, they would retreat after they found out he was in the ministry. It was almost like he had the plague; men ran and women flocked. He had more women who were "told" by God that he was supposed to be their husband. The funny thing is that God never related any such message to him. So for now, he just needed a friend, and Brian seemed like he wasn't easily intimidated.

But Brian shifted his weight uncomfortably from one foot to the other and said, "No, it's not because you are a preacher. It's just God hasn't really been one of my top priorities lately. And it doesn't seem like I am on his list of priorities, either" answered Brian. "Well It's not too late; there is no time like the present." said Max. "Maybe if I am still in town, I can hopefully come. "Well, if you are still in town, will you come?"

"You drive a hard bargain, preacher man. I will come if I am in town." Brian looked at the flier Max had handed him and tossed it on his bed and organized the rest of the boxes.

Max looked at Brian and chuckled. This man had no clue the anointing that was on his life, and he was glad God had let him be a part of helping this man put the pieces together.

~

Shirley could hear the muffled cries coming from Nicole's room as she stood outside the door and debated whether to go in or just keep walking. She had enough going on in her life without the "extras" of anyone else. Curiosity got the best of her as she knocked quietly and proceeded to crack open the door. Nicole was sitting there on the bed, drenched in tears. "Are you okay?" Shirley asked.

"Everything is all wrong. My mother won't talk to me and my baby's daddy says the baby is not his. He said he heard some of his so-called friends saying I slept with them." said Nicole.

"Well, kid, you can do one of two things. Number one, you can allow everyone else to dictate what your life will be like. Number two, you can take control of you and your baby's future and start making better decisions that are good for you and your baby." Shirley answered. "When it comes to it, Nicole, that is what being a mother is all about -- making the best decision for your child.," concluded Shirley.

"Can I ask you a question?" asked Nicole. Shirley nodded her head and Nicole continued. "Why don't you have any children? You seem like you would be an excellent mom."

Shirley took a little time to collect her thoughts; she could feel the lump of tears surfacing. "I want children, but I haven't been able to have them. I gave birth to a girl years ago, but I haven't been blessed yet. But one day, it is coming, and I'll have my miracle." said Shirley, forcing a smile to try to lighten the mood. "Until then, we need to get you together. What plans do you have?" asked Shirley. "I'm not sure; I will graduate in May. My chances of scholarships used to be great because my grades were pretty good. Now, I'm not sure because I've missed a lot of school. And how am I going to go to college with a baby…" Nicole trailed off. What was she thinking? Why did she allow herself to dream that she could be anything she wanted to be like she was some rich honor society kid filling out college applications! The truth of the matter was, no one wanted her; she would never know what it was like to open up an acceptance letter, and she could not possibly be a mom to somebody…. She couldn't even take care of herself! What was she going to do? Myles did not want to have anything to do with this child. And she was not ready to be a single mom. Was she making the wrong choice? What if her parents were right? What if she really was going to screw up this baby's life?

Shirley looked at her and felt overwhelming love for her. She walked over and hugged her tight and said, "Listen, Nicole, you are capable! Trust God, listen for his voice, and he will answer." she said.

"Maybe not in the way you think." she said with a chuckle, "but he does care for you."

"Why do people always say that? Why do they act like God really cares for me? No! God doesn't talk. At least, he never talks to me! How do you know it's God and not just what you want to hear?" challenged Nicole. "I'm a screw up; I've messed up my life, Myles's life, and our baby's life. Why would God talk to me? I don't believe in God anymore…How do you know God is real?

"I know because God made Himself real to me." Shirley answered. I've heard God too many times in my own life to deny Him. I know that my experiences mean absolutely nothing to you until you have an encounter with God yourself …. but ask God to make himself real to you, and He will. In the meantime, let's take it one day at a time." said Shirley as she hugged Nicole, knowing it must be scary at sixteen becoming a mom. Shirley smiled. God already knew she would help Nicole. God had already made Himself real to Nicole by sending Shirley to help her, and she didn't even know it. Shirley was tired, and she finally lay down to get some much-needed rest. The rest of the next couple days were a blur.

The phone rang, and it was Kathleen: "Girl, where have you been? I have been calling you for two days. What time is it?" "It's 7:30 a.m." "Dang, don't pregnant women require sleep?" asked Shirley. "Why are you up so early?" she said. "What's the matter?" said Kathleen, a little too loud for Shirley's taste. It was too early in the morning for all this drama.

"What do you want Kathleen?" "What are you saying, you don't have time for your bestest friend in the whole wide world or for the mother of your God child?" asked Kathleen, seemingly hurt. "God-child? I never agreed to that! Dealing with you is enough!" said Shirley playfully. "Hey, if I didn't know you better, I would be offended." "Open the door, I'm outside and I have an armful of food." said Kathleen. "Well, since you have food, disregard everything I just said." chuckled Shirley as she got up to open the door. "Whew, those were heavy." she said as she slammed the bags down on the countertop, and almost toppled down. "Be careful, my homeowner insurance doesn't cover psychotic pregnant women," said Shirley.

"Now my feelings are hurt." said Kathleen. "If I didn't know better, I would think that you don't love me anymore. So, how did your date go?" she asked cautiously. "Oh, it was fine," she said, trying to hide her excitement. And before she knew it, she had spilled everything. She was talking so fast that Kathleen sat down at the table in an attempt to follow along with the story. "What do you think, Kat?" said Shirley as she took a deep breath. It was the only breath she had taken since she had started telling the story. "Girl, I think you have finally gone crazy. You are saying you saw an angel and talked to God all in the same day, and you were awake for all this?" said Kathleen jokingly.

"Whatever, Kathleen, I know what happened. Now you got jokes. I am not crazy. Shirley said.

"Well, I guess you don't want to know that I went to see Gwendolyn." said Kathleen. "No, you didn't! Don't tell me you went up there, acting a fool." she said. "Me, act a fool? Why, I never!" said Kathleen with enough theatrics that could have won her an academy award. "Well, what happened?" asked Shirley, by this time curiosity had won over logic.

"Well, I was right; Brian and she never had an affair. She went through this whole 'I'm looking for God's purpose in my life' scenario." Shirley looked at Kathleen, wondering if Gwendolyn had actually had something happen, a "God experience." That definitely didn't sound like the Gwen she was used to. "Maybe she has changed." she said "You have got to be kidding; you are buying that crap?" asked Kathleen, as though she could not believe that Shirley was actually entertaining the idea. "Gwen may have changed, and good for her! But what does this mean for you and Brian?" asked Kathleen.

"Wow, now what do you want me to say -- that that changes everything?" asked Shirley. "You want me to run right over to Brian and tell him to come home? No, not this time! I know that I can't put this marriage together by myself. But I do know one thing -- I have a promise from God, and I am going to trust him. By the way, can you take me to get my car?" asked Shirley, hoping to change the subject.

"What…are you kidding? You left it at the restaurant all this time?" asked Kathleen. "What have you been doing?

She asked. "Not that it's any of your business, Shirley said with a laugh, but I have been catching up on some much needed rest...until you interrupted me. Anyway, I need to go pick up the car because I have to be in court tomorrow at 4:00 p.m." "Oh, yeah!" she said as she stuffed a spoonful of strawberry ice cream in her mouth. "So, what happens now?" Kathleen said, not bothering to finish the ice cream in her mouth before speaking.

"Are you seriously eating that junk early this morning? And stop talking with your mouth full." said Shirley. "Yes, mother." said Kathleen as she rolled her eyes. "So is this the day?" she continued.

"Yes, it appears so." said Shirley quietly. "What are you going to do?" asked Kathleen. "I am going to let go and let God." said Shirley.

Brian taped the last box and then looked around the room; Man, what a difference. The room looked bare and lifeless. The painted walls were the only indicator that this had once been someone's home.

His lawyer had been angry when he had told him that he was not going to force her to sell the house or the business that they had created together. It was Shirley who had spent the most time booking appointments and gathering the resources needed to cater the events, and she was good at her job. Yeah, in the early years they had worked together, but when he landed the job at the law firm, his contributions were pretty scarce and when he had started freelancing, he had some time. But by that time all they did was exist together. Isn't that crazy? Someone who had once been his best friend now was a total stranger to him, and he spent more time at galleries than at home.

Well, pretty soon all this would be behind him. He looked around the room to see a metal box underneath his futon. He had forgotten the lock box with his gun. He had bought the revolver for target shooting and really had never used it. He took it out but for what? He had no clue. That's odd, he thought. It's loaded. That is when the first thought occurred to him -- he would never really be free; life without Shirley was not worth living. "You can end all this madness right now," said the voice. He looked around the room, startled, and there in the corner, was a shadow. It looked like a man with a trench coat and hat. "Who are you?" asked Brian

"You already know who I am; you summoned me here. I am death." said the voice. "And I have come to help you; I understand it's just too much for you. And I have the answer: just pull the trigger." said the shadow. "And everything will be over just like that." "Oh, My God!" said Brian. "Why are you calling God? He hasn't done anything for you; that's why you need me to help you." said the raspy voice. Shadows began to creep in underneath the door and swirl around in the room. Now Brian was officially freaked out. Brian picked up the phone. Who could he call? "He was going crazy; then he looked at the bed and lying there was the flyer. He scooped up the flyer, his heart pounding so bad his head hurt. The gun was in his right hand; it was like he couldn't put it down, the pull was so strong. It was like a magnet was forcing the gun to his mouth; he gasped for breath; he was slowly being overpowered. He struggled to dial the number; his eyes were so blurry he could barely make out the numbers. He dialed slow and steady, knowing that this was his only opportunity to get help.

The phone finally started ringing: "Hello, this is Max" said the voice. "Max, this is Brian. I need your help; I didn't know who else to call." "What's going on, Brian?"

he asked. "It's over man, death is here and I don't know what to do!" exclaimed Brian. "Hang on, Brian, I'm leaving the church. I am less than ten minutes away, just keep talking." said Max. I don't think I am going to make it; can you please tell Shirley I'm sorry." said Brian. As the phone dropped, he couldn't fight anymore. It was like the shadows were closing in on him. He stopped struggling long enough to see the shadow guide his hand to his mouth, and he could feel its finger forcing his finger to pull the trigger. The coldness of the steel shocked his skin; he struggled again when faced with the reality of death. He realized he was not ready to die. "Jesus, Please help me," he cried as he sank to his knees.

Gwendolyn was not prepared at all for what she walked in on. She and Linda had been passing by Brian's house on the way to meet Alan, Linda's fiancé, for lunch to show him the designs for the wedding and formally pick out the invitations. Gwen suddenly got this strange panicked feeling that something was wrong. It was like something else had taken control of the steering wheel; she swerved and stopped in front of his house. She really did not know why she was here, but she could not ignore the sick feeling she had rising up in her stomach. "What are you doing?" asked Linda as she caught the horrified look on Gwen's face. "I don't know." she said almost as if in a trance. It was like everything had slowed down for a brief moment as she leaped out of the car, not bothering to shut the door and walked as fast as she could to his door. She knocked on the door, no answer. She wasn't sure why she felt such a sense of urgency. "Brian!" she screamed, her stomach felt like it was twisted in a million knots. Still, she got no answer, and she turned the knob to find that the door was open. The house was so cold; it sent chills instantly throughout her body.

There was a steady stream of her breath trailing in front of her as she walked. "Brian," she yelled as she frantically ran through the house, looking for him. Then she heard the gun shot as it resonated through the apartment. When she entered the room, Brian was face down on the bedroom floor in a pool of blood.

Chamber five

Shirley picked up the phone; she couldn't deny the inevitable any longer. She hoped her sister was not bothering her for nonsense because right about now she was not in the mood. She dialed her sister's number. "Hello, this is Camille," answered a seemly irritated voice on the line. Shirley took a breath and then said "Hello, Camille what do you want?"

"Oh my God, Shirley, what took you so long to call? Mama is so sick; I thought you should know she didn't want me to call you, but I just thought you should know." Shirley could hear the panic in Camille's voice. "They want to move her to Hospice. It's so bad, Shirley, I don't know what I am going to do with Mama! I tried to take care of her; I took only gigs in town, but now time is running out. I'm thirty-six; my modeling career is questionable. Shirley, I can't do this anymore. I'm going to lose my career." Shirley swallowed the lump that was in her throat. "How long have you known, Camille?" There was a long pause. "What?" she asked. "How long, Camille?" not bothering to hide her annoyance.

"A little over three years; they did surgery and removed a cyst from her ovary, but now it has spread, and there is nothing they can do." she said, and instantly burst into tears as she tried to explain: "It wasn't my fault! Mama didn't want to worry you. I wanted to tell you, but she made me promise. Please don't be mad. I need you. I can't go through this by myself."

Shirley knew that her Mama probably preferred her to be contacted after she was already dead. Most people, when faced with death, wanted to make amends with their family and friends, but not her mother! Nothing had changed. They all knew, everyone knew, but her and now that time was running out. Things needed to be done, and Mama needed to be taken care of so, of course, now they called her. She took a deep breath, and then to her relief her phone beeped. "Hold on, Camille, another call is coming through. Even though she heard Camille protest, she needed time to get herself together.

~

Linda had rushed into the house after she heard the gunshot. "Oh, my God!" she said as she saw Gwendolyn standing panic stricken in the middle of the room, staring down at Brian's body lying on the floor. Instantly, her instincts began to click in; the years of serving as a R.N. in the emergency room had helped prepare her for this very moment. She yelled for Gwen to call 911 as she instantly went to work checking for his vitals; he had a faint heartbeat. She saw that the bullet had exited the back of his skull. She worked quickly to gather as much information as she could for the paramedics so that it would be a smooth transition. She tried to stop the bleeding as much as she could, but the back of his head looked really bad. She wasn't sure that there was much that she could do. "Lord, sweet Jesus please guide my hands and help me save his life." she prayed. The sirens blared in the background and pretty soon the room was filled with policemen, ambulance drivers, and paramedics. Linda and Gwendolyn stood there in a daze as the paramedics wheeled Brian out and into the ambulance. Brian was going to have a lot of hurdles to cross if he did pull through this; the lasting damage on his brain at this point didn't look too good. Living was only half of the battle for Brian.

Max pulled up to the curb in front of Brian's house quickly and jumped out of his car, somehow in his hustle forgetting to put his car in park. He hurriedly jumped back into the car, unfortunately not before the car rolled forward hitting the car in front of him. He quickly scribbled a note and put it on the windshield. He scanned the area looking for someone who could give him information on Brian. He saw an officer draping the yellow tape and securing the area. "Oh God, please," his soul cried out on Brian's behalf. "Let him be okay." "I'm sorry you cannot come back here," said the officer as Max attempted to get as close as he could to find out what had happened. Max saw two women giving statements to the officers standing by the front door. He knew he wasn't going to be able to get any information from the attending people, so he decided to wait and talk to the women. It seemed like forever; then he finally saw the officer give them a card, and the women began to walk toward their car.

"Hello. My name is Max, and I just wanted to let you know that I accidentally ran into the back of your car. I left my insurance information and my number if you have any questions." The women nodded; he could tell they were in a daze, so he knew he would have to explain everything again later when everything had settled down. "So, how is Brian? I was on the phone with him…" his voice trailed off; he didn't want to assume the worst, but from the looks on their faces, the situation seemed pretty bad. "Hello, my name is Linda, and this is Gwendolyn; you said your name was? "Max," he answered quickly.

"Brian is in pretty serious condition." she said and then turned her attention to an officer that was approaching them. "Ladies, they are taking him to St. Rose hospital," he said and then briefly glanced at Max. "Who are you?" he questioned. "Um, I am a friend of Brian's." he said, not

127

liking the accusing look on the officer's face. "Has his wife
been contacted?" asked Gwendolyn. "Yes, she's been made
aware of the situation." the officer said nonchalantly and
walked away.

~

"Hello," said Shirley, waiting for the caller to say
something. "Hello, is this the wife of Brian Hopkins?"
"Yes, it is." she said. He went on to tell her that Brian was
at St. Rose Hospital, and they needed her to come down as
soon as possible. He didn't give her much information,
only that it was imperative that she come right away. Her
hands were shaky; it must be pretty bad if they wouldn't
tell her anything she clicked back over to Camille. "Look, I
am going to have to call you back." Shirley said. "What,
what am I supposed to do with Mama in the meantime?"
asked Camille. "I don't know what to tell you; right now, I
am going to see what is going on with my husband.
Something's happened." said Shirley, trying not to panic.
"You know, she's your Mama too. And I have to leave for
Italy in two weeks. What am I supposed to do? I have done
it for three years; it's somebody else's turn." said Camille,
revealing that she was still the same self-centered brat that
she had been when they were kids. Here she was, telling
her something was wrong and yet everything was about
Camille. "Look, I don't have time for this right now; I will
talk to you later." she said as she slammed down the phone
and hurried out the door to head to the hospital, only
stopping long enough to dial Kathleen on her cell as she
hurried to her car.

Kathleen had finally gotten Shirley to calm down long
enough to tell her that Brian was being taken to St Rose
Hospital. When she reached the hospital, she saw Shirley

pacing the hallway floor. "What's going on, Shirley?" "Brian has been shot; I don't know much more than that." she said. "I had to sign for him to have surgery; they said it will be about two hours before they will know the extent of his injuries." She was so nervous her hands were shaky as she reached out for Kathleen. "What am I going to do if he doesn't make it?" she said as she laid her head against Kathleen's shoulder. "He is going to be okay, Shirley." Kathleen said. Then she saw Gwendolyn and two other people with her. "What's she doing here?" she said, not bothering to hide her contempt for Gwendolyn.

Gwen, not wanting to start any battles, quickly addressed her question to Shirley: "How is Brian?" Shirley took a long breath and almost seemed as if she was deciding whether she should answer her or not; then she said slowly, "He is in surgery, why are you here?" Then she dropped her head; she didn't have the energy to deal with this right now.

"This is not the time or the place for us to talk, but I called the paramedics." said Gwen, hoping to dispel some of the negative emotions beginning to be generated.

"Well, I have no idea why you are here, but you are welcome to leave." said Kathleen candidly. "Who are you," she asked as she pointed to Max. "Um, my name is Max. I was on the phone with Brian. Kathleen looked like she wanted to say something else but paused when an officer approached them. "Excuse me" said the officer.

"Which one of you is the wife of Brian?" He looked around at the three ladies waiting for a response. "I am." said Shirley, dazed. "Come with me; we need to talk." Shirley grabbed Kathleen's hand and pulled her close to her, letting her know she did not want to go by herself. "It's okay; it's just routine questions. You can come with her.," he said as he nodded in Kathleen's direction. Leading them into a room where the psychologist and another doctor sat waiting.

"I didn't get the impression she was happy to see us." said Linda. "If I were her, I wouldn't be too thrilled to see me either." said Gwendolyn with a nervous chuckle. Why was she here? To tell the truth, she really had no idea. Although she couldn't convince herself to leave, she knew that it was going to be uncomfortable. After all, everyone saw her as the other woman. "Brian is part of the history I left behind if you know what I mean."

Max looked at Linda as she nodded. Evidently, Brian was somehow linked to Gwendolyn, and now he had to admit he was curious, but he thought he'd better mind his own business. He had to admit Brian had turned out to be more work than he originally intended. He thought he might be better off switching the subject. So he said, "Um, this may not be the right time, but I need to give you my insurance information so that you can get your car fixed." he said to Gwen. "What are you talking about?" she asked. "Well, I forgot to put my car in park, and it hit the back of your car and scratched your bumper." he said. Max felt like such an idiot! Who forgets to put their car in park? "I was just so nervous," he said, as he tried to explain. "Brian called me, talking about death, and I just panicked." "It's okay," she said softly. "It's just a car, and that's what we pay insurance for." she said and smiled at him.

Shirley could not believe what they were telling her. Surely, not Brian -- he would never try to kill himself, would he? Shirley felt bombarded all at once. She needed time to regroup. She excused herself from the conversation. She muttered something inaudible even to herself. Kathleen looked a little alarmed when she got up to leave; she assured her that she was okay and she just needed to go to bathroom. Shirley quickly escaped the room and retreated to the bathroom stall and just sat there. She needed to collect herself; she felt like it was all too much. She felt the cry rising up from her belly. She tried to keep her composure, but she couldn't and she let go. She didn't understand any of this; nothing even remotely resembled what her life had once been.

"Lord, I know what you said. Brian is coming home, and I thank you for the strength to endure all of this. I don't feel strong, Lord, but Your word says that I can do all things through Christ Jesus who strengthens me." She sat there until she heard a knock on the stall door. "Honey, are you okay?" said a small voice.

"Yes, I will be." she said as she opened the stall door and went to the sink to wash her face. The voice came from a little old lady. She was so cute; she looked like the grandma that everyone wished they had. The lady turned around and kind of startled her when she said, "You may think this is crazy, or I am crazy, and it's okay if you think I am crazy, but God told me to come in here and pray with you. I don't know what you are going through, but I was on my way to visit my son, and God spoke to me and told me to go into the bathroom and there would be a woman there in a stall and pray with her. Honey, you are special and God loves you." Shirley stood there staring at this woman; she was not sure she had ever heard anyone other than herself who admitted to hearing God speak, other than the people who misconstrued God's voice who were indeed hearing from Satan to do horrible things.

Who was this woman? She was so amazed at the light that followed this woman; it was almost like a glow that overcame her when she spoke. Shirley wasn't sure who this woman was, but she was sure of one thing: God had sent her to speak into her spirit and sure needed some encouragement; she needed things to get better, starting with her. She had learned that nothing was impossible with God. And she was beginning to believe that God really loved her. The woman took her hands and began praying for her; it was like there was an exchange of something. It almost felt like being jolted with electricity, nothing too drastic but not subtle enough to be ignored. This little lady prayed so hard. Pretty soon, it seemed like the little bathroom was overflowing with the spirit of God. Shirley was overwhelmed by the love she felt. God did not need her to pray to him; she needed to pray so that her focus could shift from one of defeat to understanding that with God, anything is possible.

"Honey, you are going to be okay, and your husband is going to live and he will preach the word of God. Woman of God, go forth and declare the word of the Lord over your husband. God will be your light; the joy of the Lord will be your strength; the storm is not over, but God will keep you in the midst of the storm."

Shirley felt so small underneath the power of God.

"Who am I that God continues to provide my every need?" she asked.

"You are a woman of God, and you are precious in his sight." This little lady hugged her and left her as she stood there, standing in the bathroom shaking, scared and unsure of anything, but deep inside Shirley knew she was going to be okay. Right now, she would still need to deal with the hassles of life, but now she felt like she was strong enough to stand.

~

She had the most beautiful smile. No way, it couldn't be, could it? Was she really "his" Gwendolyn, the young girl who had stolen his heart years ago? She was all grown up, but she still had that beautiful smile. "Do you know who I am?" he asked. "Yes, you are Max." said Gwen, wondering what in the world he was getting excited about. "Gwen, it's me, Max!" he said as he grabbed her by her arm. She looked at him and then she started laughing. "Oh, my goodness, Max? Is it really you?" She jumped on him with her legs straddling his waist. He twirled her around; they looked like two little kids.

"Okay, you both have gone absolutely crazy." said Linda, wondering what she had been left out of. "Linda, this is my best friend in the whole world," Gwen said with tears streaming down her face. "If you say so," said Linda, "I'm going to get some coffee. Anybody else want something?" Max and Gwendolyn were so busy talking that neither seemed to hear her; she just laughed and began her own little mystery of finding the cafeteria. "Max, I'm so sorry. I have thought about you so much throughout the years." She had never talked to him again since that horrible day at the hospital when she had lied and said Max was the dad of the baby she had aborted. Why had she panicked, why didn't she stand up and tell everyone that Shawn had raped her! Max was her only friend, and she had betrayed him.

Gwen had that sick feeling begin to rise in her stomach again. It seemed like so long ago, but the memory was so vivid; it was literally like it was unfolding right in front of her. She dropped her head in shame as she remembered.

She would never forget the tears that had welled up in Max's eyes when the nurse took her back to perform the procedure. "Gwen, it's okay, you were only fifteen; you were a baby and it was not your fault," he said gently as he lifted her head up to meet his gaze. She was still so beautiful. He could never forget her, even after all these years. He had never loved anyone as much as he loved her.

She still had that same fire in her eyes as she had when she was young. Max had loved her the day he laid eyes on her. She was only five, and he was seven when his family had moved in next door to hers. He used to wonder why someone who was so beautiful was always sad. They instantly became friends, and they were inseparable until his dad sent him to a Christian Boarding School. It had been pretty rough at first because it was the middle of his senior year and he had left the boarding school and had received a scholarship for Seminary. Here he was now, being groomed for his grandfather's church.

He had thought he had everything under control, but now seeing her, he could feel the anger rising in his heart. How could that bastard do such horrible things to a child? He took a long breath and tried to keep his poise as he listened to her apologize again for something that was not her fault.

"Max I am so sorry, I thought I would never get a chance to talk to you, and now that you are standing here, I don't know what to say except, 'Please forgive me. Please don't hate me.'" She hated not being in control; this had been an emotional day, and she felt like she had been run over by a semi-truck.

Hate her? How could she think that he could ever hate her? He loved her; even now he was surprised at how protective he felt about her. "Lord, I don't know what You are doing, but please don't let me lose her again," he prayed.

Max couldn't believe he was standing here in front of Gwen. He had often prayed for her and had even tried to find her, but her mom had told him she hadn't seen Gwen in years, and her mom had been killed a couple of years later. He had since then accepted the fact that he would probably never see her again, and there she was, standing in front of him. What are the chances of that?

Shirley sighed with relief when the doctor told her that Brian was stable. After that, she didn't understand anything else…he said something about Brian being in a coma and flying in another doctor to do neurological tests to see what injuries his brain may have sustained. "Can I see him?" she asked. She just needed to see him for herself -- all these medical terms meant nothing to her. She needed to let Brian know that she was here and everything was going to be okay.

"I don't see why not. He is in recovery right now, so it will be at few hours until he is moved; we would like to keep a close eye on him. You can have five minutes with him," said the doctor with a wink. "I have to warn you, he will have to have additional work, some of which is cosmetic, but I know you have strong faith and God can do what us doctors can't." Shirley was relieved the doctor was a fellow believer; she didn't think she had ever met a humble doctor -- most were filled with the "god syndrome", you know, the thought that life or death was in their hands. Shirley took a deep breath, said a short prayer and tried to prepare herself, but Shirley was not at all prepared for what she felt when she walked into the room. No, she wasn't prepared for the fear that gripped her heart when she was sure that she had lost him forever, and, you know what? All the months of fights and arguments seemed pointless when she saw him lying there. For the first time, right or wrong didn't matter when she saw him fighting to stay alive. She used the short precious minutes she had to quote the word of God over him and to command Satan to loose her husband. He had picked the wrong man to mess with; this man belonged to God, and she suddenly got mad. Pity time was over; she was on a mission to get back what belonged to her.

Brian lay there. He didn't know when the separation happened, but now, as he stood there watching himself sleep, he was kinda freaked out but he had calmness about him. He looked around the room, and he saw Shirley holding his hand and praying. She looked like a little doll. Standing there, she was so beautiful; he placed his hand on her shoulder; he could see she was struggling to fight back the tears. "It's okay," he said. Her heart was breaking, and it was his fault. Why had he let everything get so out of control? He didn't even know, truthfully, when his life had started its downward descent. What was he supposed to do now?

All he wanted to do was to let her know it was going to be okay. He struggled unsuccessfully to get her attention. "Shirley," he called out, but she was unaware of his presence. She was standing there staring at the shell of which his soul had long yet departed. He was not ready to die, and yet he didn't think he knew how to live. Maybe everyone was better off without him; he saw so much pain in her eyes, the one whom he had chosen to love, to cherish, and to honor. And do you know what the hardest thing to swallow about this situation was? To know that he caused the majority of Shirley's pain. He had really messed up.

"You really made a mess of things, didn't you?" said a voice. He whirled around, and there stood Danny. "Danny, is it really you?" Brian realized he must have gone totally insane, or was he dead? That's the only thing that would make sense: Danny was already dead, and now he was dead, too.

"Danny, is it really you?" Brian said with a whisper. He was almost afraid to speak. What in the world was going on? Was he having a hallucination, or was Danny really here?

"Yeah, it sure is, and I want to know one thing -- what in the world are you doing to yourself?" Danny stood only a few feet away from Brian; he looked just as he had before the accident. "I need to hear an explanation as to why you are messing up your life?" "Danny, is it really you?" said Brian again. "Yes, it's me, and I want you to tell me what are you doing?"

"Danny, things are bad, and I don't know if I can fix it." Brian stammered.

"What are you doing man, are you giving up?" Danny looked so real he didn't look like a ghost. Wasn't he supposed to be glowing or something?

Brian walked slowly over to Danny and reached his hand out and touched his shoulder. He didn't know really what he expected, but as he touched Danny's shoulder, it felt real enough. Brian didn't even know where to begin; it felt like he had thousands of thing bottled up on the inside and, oddly enough, just for a moment, this was the closest to normal his life had been in a long time. He took a long pause and then carefully said, "When you died, it was like everything fell apart. I didn't know one day from the next. I am moving out of the house, telling the only woman I have ever loved that I need a break and then next thing I know, I almost had an affair, Danny. Shirley and me are getting a divorce. What am I supposed to do? I can't live without her. Maybe God should have done us both a favor and taken me instead of you!" Now that he had finally admitted it, deep down inside Brian felt like God had made a mistake somehow. He had to admit he felt better; he had never had the courage to admit that he had given up right there in the heap of the mangled metal where his best friend had died.

"Brian, my time was up. I had accomplished my

purpose, and through my daughter I will live. Man, you have so much to live for; don't forget why you live and for whom you live."

"That's the problem -- I don't know who I live for; I don't know why I live, don't you understand? I don't know anything, anymore." Brian was sure of one thing -- his life was spinning out of control, and there was nothing he could do. Everywhere he turned, it seemed like disaster.

"You need to get ahold of your life, and you need to get right with God, and He will help you find purpose." Danny knew that Brian felt like he was at the end of his rope, but he wanted him to see that God had a bigger purpose for him, even though he could not even imagine the greatness that was inside of him.

"God does not want me. I am a screw up. What can He possibly do with me?"

"God does not need you because you are perfect, but He is there to show Himself through you if you let Him. He can show how in your weakness in Him you find strength. You have a long road ahead of you. If you could do it all by yourself, then why would you need Him? He has called you for such a time as this, and God wants to work in your life. You will wake up, but you have a lot of hurdles to climb, and it will be frustrating. But, Brian, don't do it by yourself. Let God help you find your way up. Make this the bottom of the barrel and begin the slow climb up. You have to learn how to love yourself. Until you learn to live for God, you will not be any good for yourself or Shirley. Life is too short, and it's over, just like that. Man, it's so much bigger than just you! There is still work to be done after this life; it's not over!" Do you know how many things I would do differently with Kat, knowing what I know now? We all make mistakes, Brian, I have hurt Kathleen, too, but God is what kept us together." His voice trailed off as his eyes reflected love that had stood the test of time. "If I could hold her just one more time…I spent so much time focused on things that really now make no sense. Make it right -- that's all I have to say."

"The love I feel for Kathleen will never fade; it just changes. It's now how it was intended to be in the beginning. Your best years are still ahead of you. Brian, will you do me a favor? I have to go now. Please tell Kathleen that I love her and it's okay to be happy. I want her to live, and she will always be my 'star.' And tell her that I like the name Paige for my daughter. Here, give this to her, he said, as he pressed a gold locket into my hands. I gave him a hug and said, "Keep your head up." "Get it right man with God 'cause I want to see you again, alright?" And with that, Danny was gone. "Danny, don't leave yet!" He frantically searched the room, looking for any signs of Danny, but he was gone. There were still so many things that Brian didn't get to say, so many questions left unanswered. He stood there once again looking at Shirley; she looked so frail and tired. But he could see the fire in her eyes; she was walking around the room, quoting scriptures. This woman was fighting for his life.

"Lord, I am tired of doing this on my own I need You! Where are You? You promised that you would never leave me, but why do I always feel alone?" he sobbed. Brian was at the end of his rope. He had done it his way; now he was ready to do it God's way, and if He would have him, he was ready to come home. There was a knowing in his heart that God was somehow speaking to him. It wasn't a loud audible voice, but it was almost as if God had somehow ushered him into His throne room, and right now he didn't feel like a grown man, he felt like a little boy who just needed to be picked up and loved by his Father. His soul ached for God, and it was filled as he felt a pulling in his spirit as he was slowly guided toward his body. Lying on the table, he felt like a force was compelling him to the lifeless body, and it was almost like he was thrown back into the body. He gasped for air. Machines were going off left and right, and doctors were pouring into the room as his body began to tremble out of control almost as if he was having a seizure. The nurses ushered Shirley out of the room. The panic look on her face would be etched in his memory for a long time. Brian looked over and saw the angels standing around his table directing the doctors, and he knew he was going to be okay.

Kathleen waited as long as she could in the emergency waiting room, but enough was enough; somebody was going to tell her something. Patience was a virtue she was working on. She stood up and walked toward the nurses' desk and could see the lady working the desk doing her best to look distracted, as this was around the twentieth time she had tried unsuccessfully to get information. Just as Kathleen was about to resort to drastic measures, she saw Shirley running toward her with a horrified look on her face: "What is it, Shirley?" She felt the fear grip her heart: "Oh my God, please let Brian live." she prayed as she waited for Shirley to catch her breath.

"He just had a really bad seizure, and I don't know, Kat, it looks really bad. Shirley sobbed. She looked so small, not the superhero that she was so many times before. Right now, Shirley needed God to work a miracle. "It's me, Lord, I need you." she said as she collapsed against Kathleen shoulder to find the strength she needed. They stood for what seemed like an eternity when they were interrupted by a voice, "Excuse me, Mrs. Hopkins?" said a young doctor who didn't look old enough to have finished high school. But he was supposed to be the great neurologist that was flown in to assess Brian's injuries. "Yes, sir, I am Mrs.

Hopkins," said Shirley, racing toward the "kid wonder." It looked like she was holding her breath. He smiled slightly, trying to reassure her. "My name is Dr. Martin. First, I would like to tell you that Brian is fine. He woke up; the seizure you witnessed was probably very scary, but I want you to know that it is a natural response to a patient who has had so much head trauma.

Now, Mrs. Hopkins, I cannot tell you that he has not suffered any memory loss or even to what extent his injuries are or even the lasting effect of this on him, but he sure remembers you. He has been asking for you since he regained consciousness. I should warn you that over the next couple of days, we may have to induce him into a coma-like state so that we can further assess his injuries. But as for now, he seems to be somewhat stable; asking for you is a pretty good sign."

Shirley breathed a sigh of relief; he was back! Any form of Brian was better than losing him altogether.

~

Gwendolyn and Max had seen a lot of each other since that horrible day at the hospital. She always tried to make sure that there were lots of people around; she did not trust herself to be alone with him. It was crazy because she felt for him something she had never felt for anyone; it was the closest to love she had ever come. She had invited him, along with Linda and her fiancée Alan, over for dinner. Why, she had no clue, truthfully; she just needed to be with Max, and yet she was afraid to even be in the same room as him. She didn't know what to say, but something about being with him was natural.

"So, Gwendolyn, how did you guys meet?" asked Linda.

"We were next-door neighbors." answered Gwen. "We were only kids; I was five and he was seven and we were inseparable for a long time." Gwen's voice kinda trailed off as she was painfully reminded as to why they had been separated. Max, seeing that far away pained look in her eyes, grimaced; he hated talking about their past, but it was their only connection. Only the bad memories were so intertwined with the good that it was almost impossible to remember one without the other, and yet, that's all they had, memories of what could have been if what shouldn't have happened could have been avoided. If there was anything Max could have done, somehow he would have protected her and truthfully he had blamed himself a long time because he felt like such a coward. He should have spoken up and let everyone know what Shawn was doing to her. Gwendolyn was forced to deal with the aftermath of the rape all by herself and the abortion that had almost killed her. He had taken the easy way out; going to boarding school was a piece of cake compared to Gwen's life.

"Wow, you guys have known each other some years," said Alan. And the whole table erupted into laughter when Linda said, "So, what you trying to say my friend is old?" Alan scrambled for words to say and finally just sat back and laughed when he realized he had unknowingly stuck his foot in his mouth. Gwendolyn was glad that the tension had been broken, and she bounced up to get the pie she had baked from the kitchen.

Brian smiled when he saw Shirley peer into the room, and he was filled with joy when her eyes lit up when he called her name. He felt like he had a million things to say, but he quickly became frustrated when he realized nothing would come out; his once smooth voice spilled out in slow robotic rhythms. And all that he struggled to say came out in gurgling inaudible sounds which made no sense to him because he could fully understand what he was saying himself, but her puzzled look let him know something was lost in the translation. Shirley poured some water; he could see her hands trembling as she nervously brought it to her mouth as she glanced at the doctor who walked into the room holding a stack full of papers. "Hello, how are we doing this morning?" he said to Brian. Brian closed his eyes as he felt the tears escaping. He was in pain, and he was exhausted. "And how are you, Mrs. Hopkins?" "I am doing fine, Dr. Martin. So, can Brian come home sometime soon?" Shirley asked. She did not like the way he seemed to avert his eyes whenever she asked him about Brian coming home.

"Well, let's slow down a little. I would like to talk to you about the test, can you come with me?" Shirley walked slowly behind the Doctor; she knew from his face and his tone she was not going to like what he was going to say. She somehow felt like she was caught in a really bad dream. Soon she would awaken and it would all be over, but she knew it would not erase the last few weeks in her mind.

Brian did not like the fact that they were discussing his results without him. But it was all well and good; he didn't know if he could handle another bad test result. The last few weeks had been grueling; he had endured test after test and truthfully he was tired but he was mostly irritated. The things he used to be able to do with minimal effort now took every ounce of energy he had. He lay there for a long time, caught between sleep and his horrible reality of life.

Shirley stood there in disbelief as the doctor calmly explained to her that Brian would probably need to be moved into a rehabilitation center. "It's best for Brian, Shirley. I know you think that you can do it by yourself, but he is going to require a lot of attention, and truthfully I think this is the best option for him and you, too." What was he talking about? There was no way that she was going to let him go into a rehab center; he needed to be at home with his wife. "I am capable of giving him whatever care he needs; his insurance will pay for a home nurse, and I will learn whatever I need to learn."

"Mrs. Hopkins, I need you to know that I strongly disagree with your decision; you are making an emotionally-based decision not based on the facts, although I think it's quite noble of you to want to take him home.

What are you going to do when your help and support system fails and you are too tired to do anything for yourself? Brian may never be the same as he was before. Are you ready for all that may come as a result of his injuries?" Dr. Martin wished that she could understand he had seen this mistake made over and over; spouses of severely injured patients take them home and end up resenting the decision because their life as they know it is over. And good intentions are just not enough.
"Look, Dr. Martin, I know you are trying to do your job, but have you ever been where I am?" No one had ever asked him that question before. "Umm, what do you mean?" he asked. "Well, doctor have you ever been told to walk away from the only person you have ever loved and leave him in the care of strangers where he is going to be only a case number?"

"Well, no, Mrs. Hopkins, I have not, and I truthfully… I am not married, but I hardly see what love has to do with this."

"Well, Dr. Martin, you wouldn't because there is one thing that your textbooks don't teach you and that is that love conquers all odds. And there are some things you can't learn in a textbook."

"Well, I hope for your sake it's true; I am not too good in the love area," he said awkwardly. She looked at him with a smile and deep down he found himself fighting for her, wanting to believe that one day he would be lucky enough to experience this conquering love she talked about.

He stood there in amazement; this woman stood defiant, daring him to challenge her little theory, and she was sure she could handle anything. Love may be strong, but he couldn't help but feel that people in love seem to lose all sense of reason, trapped in a fantasy world. He looked at her and then finally gave in and said, "Well, I guess the only thing I can say is that I will help you anyway I can; maybe I will set up some in-home visits for the first couple of months until I can help you through this. There are a few classes you need to take and a few pieces of equipment, but I don't see why we can't shoot to have everything done and settled and him home in a week or so. How does that sound?" Shirley leaped forward and tightly hugged his neck; he closed his eyes and savored this moment; it was the closest he had been to a person in a long time.

Gwen tried to hint to Linda that she wanted her to stay, but she was so engrossed in Alan that she was missing all of the obvious signs. She sighed as she scooped up some leftover spaghetti in containers as she heard them mumble goodbye and shut the door. "Here, let me help you with that; you cooked, I'll clean," said Max as he ushered her to a seat in the living room. "You want some coffee?" he asked as he made himself at home in her kitchen, filling the dishwasher and washing the remainder by hand.
"Yes, I could use some," she said with a yawn as the tiredness of a stressful week began to creep up on her.

For a long time, the only noise heard was Max shuffling the dishes. Shirley curled up and fell asleep on the couch as she waited for him to finish.

Kathleen entered the hospital with an armful of flowers she was looking for Shirley when she spotted her and the Dr. in the hallway. "Hi Shirley." "Oh hi, this is Dr. Martin and this is Kathleen." "Hi, Dr. Martin, I hope Shirley is not giving you too much of a hard time." "No, she was just running down the rules of love." He immediately felt quite silly and tried to explain: "I mean, I have never been in love; well obviously you have had a lot of love!" he said, pointing to her belly and then felt even worse and just turned around and walked away quickly before he could make a bigger fool of himself.

Kathleen giggled as she handed the flowers to Shirley and gave her a hug. It was right there that Shirley had a bright idea; she smirked although it would have to wait. Her expertise was needed right now, she thought, as she turned around and walked into Brian's room, excited to tell him the good news.

Max walked out into the living room, finding Gwen sleeping peacefully. She stirred when she heard him sit down the coffee cups. "I hope you like sugar and cream," he said, as he handed her the mug with some of the best coffee she had ever tasted.

"No, it's perfect."

Max wondered what was going through her mind; there was so much about her that he knew, but yet there was so much that he had yet to learn; she was complicated, yet intriguing. "So, Gwen tell me what has been going on?" Before long, Gwen had told him every dreadful part of her life: the good, the bad, and the ugly, and he sat there spellbound, hanging on to her every detail. She felt so comfortable. When she finished, she begin to fear she had told him everything too soon. After all, he was a minister. If he was interested in her, he probably was scared off now. But he leaned forward and said, "Gwen, I need to ask you to do something." His heart was beating fast, and his palms felt clammy. His voice began to quiver; he felt like that little seven-year-old boy that he was when he had first met her. "I need you to forgive me," he said. "Forgive you for what?" she questioned. "Because I didn't protect you and if I had stood up to him, your mom probably would still be alive. I am so sorry." Max immediately felt the chill rise in the room. "What do you mean still alive. Is my mom dead?" Gwendolyn felt like she had just been kicked in her gut; she struggled to breathe. "Answer me, Max!" she frantically yelled. "I am so sorry, Gwen, I thought you knew!" He realized in horror that she had no clue. "My God, I thought you knew." He didn't know what else to say. "You thought I knew what?" she demanded. Max took a deep breath; he knew he could not exit this conversation. He was going to have to tell her everything, and he would be hurting her all over again.

~

Brian was glad that he would soon be going home, but right now he had things to do. Physical therapy had been a pain, but he forced himself to keep pressing forward. He lay there night after night practicing his words; he was able to regain the movement of most of his limbs, but he was so slow and sometimes he just felt so frustrated. But Shirley was by his side, and he felt like he could conquer anything. He remembered his conversation with Danny and asked Shirley to get Kathleen. He watched her expression as he told her what he had promised and gave her the gold locket. She had cried and told him it was the first gift Danny had given to her when they were dating; he had taken the locket just days before his death to get it inscribed. On the back it read, "Two hearts that beat in one rhythm".

He felt like it took him so long to tell her the story; he could have written it, but he wanted to tell her. "Danny says he likes the name 'Paige'." She felt so happy: "Paige, huh? I like that." she said as she embraced Brian. "Thank you so much for being Danny's friend," she said, her eyes filling with tears. "No, thank you for loving him," said Brian. "It's through your love that I have learned that love is unconditional." Dr. Martin had walked in and stood awkwardly trying to pretend he was not intruding on their display of emotion.

"Hi, sorry to interrupt this tender moment, but how is my patient today?" asked Dr. Martin. He looked around the room, wondering why he seemed to be so confident in him "the doctor" but extremely uncomfortable in himself "the human". And, to be frank, he had a hard time expressing any display of emotion. He had just about had a cow when he had to send flowers to his nurses for staff appreciation week. His sister had always said that he couldn't have everything: he was cute and smart, that would make up for his lack of feelings.

Gwendolyn sat quietly for a long time after Max told her that Shawn had brutally murdered her mother. Then she was overcome with emotion: "I hate him, I hate him, I hate him," she said as she sobbed. Max felt totally helpless; what was he supposed to do? "Lord, give me the words to say." He grabbed her and held her until the sobbing stopped. Every time Gwendolyn felt like she was getting a grip on life, something else came and she was left again struggling to catch her bearings.

Shirley and Nicole struggled to make sure everything was ready for Brian to come home. Nicole was getting closer and closer to delivery. Shirley was so glad she had stepped in and helped her so much with the catering business, and Nicole was doing quite well. The business was flourishing, and it gave her a sense of accomplishment and freed Shirley up to spend time with Brian at the hospital. She had completed her classes on specialized care; now she was just waiting for Brian to come home. Shirley had been so busy taking care of Brian; she hadn't had time to do much of anything. She heard a knock on the door, and she opened the door to find Camille standing there and sitting in a wheel chair was the frail shell of what used to be her mother. Her head was hung low to her chest; she in no way resembled the proud woman that she had once been.

"Can we come in or what?" said Camille. Shirley didn't trust herself to say anything, so she stepped back and watched them make their way toward the living room. "This is a pretty nice house," said Camille, trying to make small talk, but it was obvious that she was tired and anxious. This was not just a visit, it was a mission. She wheeled her mother in the center of the living room, locked her wheels on the chair, and flopped herself down and said, "Do you have anything cold to drink? It's pretty hot." Shirley was glad to have something to do as she busied herself, making some fresh lemonade. Was that woman really her mother? She had once been so beautiful and vibrant, and now she was being eaten by a disease that scrambled through her body and ate away at her organs. But the strangest thing is Shirley felt herself feeling sorry for her mom even though she knew her mother had nothing but contempt for her. She arranged the lemonade on a tray with three glasses and some muffins and fresh fruit; she was sure they would be hungry. She said a short prayer: "Lord, give me strength," took a deep breath, and entered into the living room.

Kathleen stared at the computer screen; she had hoped to be finished with this book already, but somehow the words seem to come less and less lately. She was losing her passion for writing. Then she had a brainstorm; she had a story happening right around her, one of love and betrayal and love and hope, faith and trust, scandal and death -- all the things that life entailed, and then she started writing. She hoped her editor would see the potential that she saw. "Tears in the Chambers of Heaven" -- this was a story that she knew about first hand; she began the character sketch and she wrote for hours, sometimes through tears, sometimes through laughter, but, most importantly, through her heart…the words flowed, healing the places in her heart that hadn't been touched in a long time.

"What do you want, Camille?" Shirley was tired of the procrastination. Camille was here for a reason, and she wanted to nix the small talk and get to the true intention for this visit. Her mom every now and then would look up, but for the most part, she seemed to be incoherent. Camille looked at Shirley and smiled. "You were never one to mince words. That's one thing I remember about you as a kid," she said. "Camille, you and I both know this is not a social visit. What do you want?" Shirley was not in the mood to reminisce.

"I need you to let mom move in for just a little while so that I can get back on the road," Camille said, barely above a whisper. Either mom didn't know Camille's plans or she was scared Shirley was going to say no. Her suspicions were confirmed when her mother irritably said, "I have cancer; that does not mean that I am deaf. I don't want to be here with her, and she doesn't want me here. Just take me home, so that I can die in peace." Camille burst into tears.

"Mama, please don't talk like that! You are going to live! You have to live Mama....I can't make it without you." It was almost as if she hadn't thought of the possibility that her mother may not pull out of this, and for the first time she looked anything but glamorous. She had big dark bags underneath her eyes. "Camille, come here," said her mother. Camille slowly walked over to her, and her mother tenderly guided her onto her lap and held her. Shirley had never seen her mother display such emotion, and she had to swallow back the tears. Her mother was "human" after all. Shirley could see the stress on her sister's face. Even though they had never really been close, she didn't deserve any of this. Neither did her mom, for that matter, but how was she going to balance Brian and Catherine?

Chamber six

Gwendolyn didn't know when she dozed off, but she awoke to the smell of sausage and eggs. She went to the bathroom and turned on the water faucet; she grimaced as she splashed the cold water on her face and tried to wash away the remnants of the hurt, pain and tears. She looked in the mirror, and her mama's eyes gazed back at her. The older she got, the more she looked like her. It was still hard for her to comprehend the fact that her mom was really gone, and the worst part about it was she had never had the chance to tell her that she loved her. She had not talked to her since that horrible day she had stabbed him and ran for her life, never looking back until now. Why hadn't she just killed him when she had the chance? If she had, her mom would have still been alive today. Why was all this stuff happening to her right now? The more she tried, the worse her life became She wasn't sure just how much more she could take! Linda was always telling her that God's hand was unchanging. Well, his hand might not be changing, but right now her life felt out of control, so whether or not his hand was or was not changing apparently had nothing to do with her! "Ok, lady time to pull it together," she mumbled as she patted the water off her face with a fluffy rose-colored hand towel. She just couldn't allow herself to fall into a pit; her last pit took too long to get out! Gwen was sure of one thing: She had felt much pain in her life, but somehow this time she knew it would be different. It had to be different…she needed this to be different.

She took a deep breath as her stomach rumbled. Suddenly, she was hungry. She found her way to the kitchen, and there stood Max. He was humming a song as he gently put his arms around her and led her to the table where he had made a pretty impressive spread. "You had better be careful Max; I might want to keep you," she said, as she hungrily devoured the food he had placed on her plate. "That is what I am banking on dear; you don't think I make my special eggs for anyone, do you?" he said with a wink. "Did you spend the night; are you allowed to do that? Isn't there something in your ethics book about spending the night with a 'strange' woman?" she said, halfway jokingly; yet, she felt a little silly as she laughed. Nervously, she glanced at him. To be honest, she wasn't sure what the rules were of dating a man of his caliber, a man of the cloth.

What was really going on? Yes, they had been together every day since the hospital, but were the fleeting moments just merely catching up on old times or could there really be something more? He just made you breakfast. Slowdown, you don't want to make the same mistake that you made with everyone else, said the little voice inside her heart. But she had to admit, she had never felt like this about anyone else. Okay, maybe she was feeling him just a little bit. But he was a man who would soon be a pastor. And when faced with the facts, even she had to admit she was not exactly "First Lady" material, whatever that meant.

She was lost in thought for a while, and then Max grabbed her shoulders and said, "Careful, don't start acting weird on me, or I'll never make eggs for you again. Then who would be there to make you breakfast?" Electricity went through her body when she felt his hands on her shoulders. She exhaled a little too loudly, and he removed his hands just as suddenly as he had placed them on her shoulders.

Oh, he felt it, alright. She had awakened something deep inside that he had never thought he would feel; it was like something dormant had been brought back to life. The smell of her skin; the softness of her hair; the fullness of her lips. God, how he longed to hold her, to forever make her his. He shook his head…he knew the battle was in the mind. And he could not afford to be entertaining fleshly thoughts. It was funny -- he had never really given marriage or family too much thought. Lately though, he had begun to realize how lonely his life had felt without Gwen. Could he have really fallen in love with her, or was he still in love with the little girl he once knew. Right now all he knew is that, this felt right. When he was away from her there was a void that used to be filled with ministry and his life crusade of helping others but he couldn't concentrate on anything lately. His grandfather had questioned him, but he dare not say anything until he was sure of where he stood with Gwendolyn. Besides, he didn't really know how she felt about him. One thing was sure -- she had, had more than her share of heartaches and he definitely did not want to be the cause of anymore hurt; so for now he would have to table how he really felt until he was sure of what she really felt. "So what is on your agenda today?" he asked. "Nothing much, I am going to meet with Linda and Alan and go over more plans for their wedding. It seems like I have been busy with everything else, and now it's time to buckle down and get to work," she said as she stuffed another piece of sausage in her mouth.

"What about you?"

"Just a couple of things at the church need my attention, and I plan on visiting Brian later I was hoping you would go with me." he paused giving her an opportunity to answer and when he saw her nod her head yes, he went on with the conversation.

"What types of things have you done for the wedding?" he asked

"Nothing you would find interesting, just details," she said. In truth, she wanted to run and get the designs and share with him this part of her life. Although at the same time she was self-conscious when it came to her work; she was outside of her element, and this was her first wedding. What if he thought her designs were horrible? She knew he wasn't going to take no for an answer. When he wanted to be, he could be pretty stubborn.

"Well, humor me. Anyway, you could see this as a mini presentation …practice…an ice breaker of sorts," he smiled his victory smile when he realized that he had worn her down. "Okay, already! If you insist, but don't blame me for boring you." Even though she pretended to be annoyed, he saw that she was more than happy that he had taken an interest in her work. She looked like a little kid almost skipping as she hurried to get the designs. For the next forty minutes he was captivated; she was amazing.

When she finally concluded, he was mesmerized by her creativity.

"So what do you think?" she said, barely breathing as she waited for his response. "Is it okay? I was trying to go for something original?" she said at last.

"Please be honest. I know these are just sketches, but it will look better in person." She felt like a little child stammering, trying to explain a picture that no one else could see.

"Gwen, it is better than okay; it's perfect." She was good; it was unlike anything he had ever seen.

"There's only one problem: I hope you kept some ideas for your own wedding," he said and immediately regretted it after she stopped dead in her tracks. "Yeah, I don't think I will ever have that problem; I am not the marrying type." she said sadly and gathered her designs and retreated out of the room.

"Way to go Max! You were doing so well," he said to himself. He could have kicked himself. Why had he just assumed that she would one day want to get married? Maybe that was a sexist comment. He had a lot of things to learn about women, and right now, one in particular made him question everything he thought he knew about her and himself included. Was she repulsed at the idea of marriage or was he presumptuous to think that maybe she had contemplated him as a candidate?

Shirley could not believe what she was doing; she must be crazy. Her mother was not so thrilled with the idea, but when faced with the cold reality that she had nowhere else to go, she slumped down defeated, pursed her lips in a pout, and glared at Camille.

Shirley excused herself and went in to prepare the room that would be her mother's dwelling place for the time being; it was a small room true enough, but she had decorated it beautifully. The colors had been inspired by many beautiful sunny days. This was one of her favorite rooms in the house. She sighed as the memories began racing through her mind. She smiled as she remembered when she and Brian had walked through this house with the agent and she could not contain her excitement; this was about the twentieth house they had looked at in six months. Somehow she knew the minute they walked in, this was the one. She had spent hours decorating, selecting every detail with meticulous taste, and now glancing around surveying her creation, none of it seemed important if she didn't have someone to share it with. When they had bought this house, their lives seemed embroidered with limitless possibilities; six bedrooms and a dream, they had planned to fill it with their children. She had even heard the laughter of their little miracles and the pitter-patter of little feet racing though the rooms, playing hide and seek.

Somehow, in the disappointments of life, she had forgotten to dream. She couldn't help but wonder if all that was left was memories that she held on to, but were they just memories contaminated with embellished fantasies? That seemed like such a lifetime ago. She wasn't even sure where she and Brian stood lately; her emotions had been all over the place. She took a deep breath and wondered how she was going to deal with her mother on top of her already added stress. Brian was doing much better than was expected, but he still was going to need more time until he was semi-normal, whatever that meant. Shirley tucked the corner of the bedspread; even the most mundane task seemed to require extraordinary strength. She felt someone staring at her, so she stopped and saw Camille standing in the doorway. Camille came and stood by the bed. "Do you need any help?" she asked. Shirley could tell that she wanted something, and really didn't feel ready to talk, but she could see Camille was making an effort.

"No, I am fine, Camille. I know things have been tough, but it's going to get better." Shirley was not used to seeing her this way; she was always the strong confident sister, always sure of what she wanted, and she stopped at nothing to get it, but she looked horrible. The once self- deemed goddess now was suddenly like everyone else, "human". "So when do you leave for your next shoot and where are you going, my dear?" said Shirley, hoping that

Camille would see she was really making an effort to be friendly.

"Shirley, I don't know, hopefully, I can get a shoot somewhere in Germany. You know, they are nicer than Americans to aging women," her lip quivered. "I am not as young and in demand as I used to be," she pouted.

"It's going to be fine; you will find work, and you will do as you always do -- you will shine." Who was this woman who stood in front of her waiting for her to give her answers to questions she never wanted to face herself. The almighty Camille had fallen to her knees, and somehow Shirley had always pictured this moment to be much different. She had envisioned the smile of contentment that would spread across her own face as she savored the moment that the "Queen Bee" had stepped down. At last, Shirley would be able to prove that she was not much different from anyone else. But as she looked at Camille, she couldn't help but feel sorry for the sister she had envied so long. Shirley felt her heart breaking for her. She was chasing a dream that ultimately was unattainable; no one could be young forever, sadly not even Camille.

Gwen stuffed her designs in the car and began the drive to the restaurant where her meeting would take place. But she couldn't help but ponder the questionable look that spread over Max's face as she had stormed out of the room Why she had overreacted, she had no clue, but she wanted to be married. She was tired of being alone. She would often glance at lovers walking by or hear them exchanging sweet nothings, and she would wonder when it was going to be her turn. Max confused her. Did they really share love, or were they pursuing a fantasy that was better left in a dream? Well, for right now she definitely didn't have time to decipher the code called love.

"No, Shirley, I don't think that it is going to be okay. For the first time in my life, I'm not sure what to do. What am I going to do without Mama? You know, it's funny; I had always seen her as invincible," said Camille. She stared at the wall and thought, considering all that Shirley had been through, could she really ask her to place herself in "another situation" that Camille herself would not have the strength to withstand? Shirley thought to herself, it had always seemed like Mama was made tough as nails! She knew that it was killing her mom to have no other option but stay with the child she so despised, the child that reminded her that life was less than perfect, littered with regrets. Shirley swallowed back tears; she knew that she was one of the biggest regrets in her mama's life. No matter how much she tried, she had made up in her mind years ago, and she had stuck to that decision not to love her! But right now the sensible one had to make the right decision. The sensible one had to love her regardless of the transpiring of events.

Shirley stopped and looked at Camille and said, "It's going to be okay; you will find work, and Mama will be well-taken care of. Don't worry."

"I will hire a full-time nurse and don't worry about if she needs anything. I will provide financially for her. There is an account set up," and she handed her a Visa card. Camille paused as she placed the card in her hand and looked in her eyes and said, "Shirley I'm sorry that Mama treated you so bad." She let her voice trail off as her eyes filled with tears.

Shirley felt the lump rising in her throat as she struggled to keep the tears from falling, but to her dismay, they tumbled down her face. "I am sorry. It must have been horrible the way she treated you ....The way I treated you, too." She actually looked sorry. Shirley caught her breath as they stood in awkward silence. "I am so sorry. Please say something." Camille looked desperate and Shirley wanted to tell her that it was okay to hug, to let go of the past hurt. How long she waited for somebody, anybody to admit that what they had done to her was wrong. All the long nights she lay crying, wishing somebody would notice that she was there. And now here she was in front of her sister, and she really wanted to let go, but something began to swell in the pit of her stomach. It burned as it tossed and turned inside her body, mutating as it began rising up, spiraling through every unhealed part in her body, festering and giving life to every past hurt. She remembered every time they had hurled accusations at her and daddy. Oh, daddy… she missed him so much. Why had he left her in so much pain? Why hadn't he stayed with her? She felt dizzy and much like she wanted to vomit.

Camille must have sensed that she had maybe taken things too fast. She began to step back with a horrified look on her face. But it was too late. The dormant volcano had been awakened, and there was not enough time to run, so she braced herself for what was to come next.

"Why Camille, why are you sorry? Is it that now you will be alone like I have been for all of these years?" Shirley didn't even know that she was so angry. Her words escaped her mouth like venom, and her sister reacted just like she had been struck by a rattler's bite. She wanted to stop when she saw the impact her words had on her sister, but a part of her didn't care what she felt. She wanted her to feel the pain that they had caused her. Camille looked stunned at first, then she back away slowly. The look of horror slowly twisted into pain. She opened her mouth as if she wanted to say something, but then decided not to and quickly turned and walked out of the room, leaving Shirley alone and humiliated.

"So, Brian you will soon be going home" stated Dr. Martin as he looked into his eyes, checking the dilation of his pupils.

"That's what you keep saying, but every day passes, and here I am! So you tell me doc, when am I going to get my wings?"

"Well, if you keep progressing then maybe another couple of days."

"Alright, I am going to hold you to that, and when I get out of here, we need to have a celebration dinner. You, me, my wife, and a really good friend of mine" said Brian with a chuckle.

"This friend wouldn't happen to be a woman would it?"

"Whatever would give you that idea?" Brian said, trying his

hardest to look innocent.

"You had better try to focus on getting yourself out of here and let me focus on my love life."

"What! Me? I am appalled that you think that I am trying to fix you up; why can't it be just a celebration of me getting my life together?"

"You know what? If I didn't know any better, then you would have almost convinced me, but I have seen that look before countless times and you know what I am going to tell you just like I told them, it won't work out. I am not the 'fixer-up type' so you work on getting better." Dr. Martin was kind of amused and kind of puzzled as to how he was on everyone's top ten lists of people to fix up. The last date he went on was a blind date, and she was a control freak and almost borderline stalker; it had taken him a long time to get rid of her. This woman was crazy; she was always sending him flowers and hanging out in the hospital, saying she was just in the neighborhood. His sister had told him he was overacting, but who tries to sleep with you on the first date? Okay, maybe he was a little old-fashioned and nowadays he had every eligible female and some who are not so "eligible" throwing themselves at him. He was a doctor, and there was no problem getting women. But he wanted the right woman, not just any woman. He was sure that he would know her when she came along and until then, he wanted to steer clear of the opposite sex. And why was everyone sweating him? Why couldn't they understand he was okay being single? After all, not everyone needed a mate to be complete, and the truth was he was surrounded with dysfunctional relationships. Truth be told, relationships just seem to complicate things, and he was complicated enough, all by himself.

~

Camille sat in her car for a long time outside of the house. What had just happened? Nothing had gone according to how she had planned it; where the rift had happened between them she had no idea. As long as she could remember, she had always been envious of Shirley, always knowing what to say, when to say it, and how to say it. Daddy had loved Shirley so much. There had been times when it seemed like he actually loved her more than Camille. It seemed ironic; she had tried so hard to relate to daddy, but they didn't seem to have anything in common. And here comes Shirley, who is like peas in a pod with daddy. She had always felt like she had to compete for his attention, and somewhere along the way she had stopped even trying. When daddy died, she had blamed Shirley because if she hadn't been so perfect in daddy's eyes, maybe she would have had a chance to get to know him.

Daddy's life had always been a revolving door, and Camille was always on the outside looking in. It wasn't until Mama got sick that she had learned about the rape. Her Mama told her everything, and then it had all made sense: the snide remarks and the way her Mama had treated Shirley. How could she let her mom say so many hurtful things to her? She had the right to be mad. After all, Shirley was her sister, and she was a kid, but even after she was grown up, she still didn't bother to stand up for her. Some big sister she was; she should have protected her. Well, today she would start and only hope it was not too late to make amends; after all, they were family.

Linda was absolutely ecstatic about Gwen's ideas for a "jazz under the stars" wedding. And if Gwen could have left before the focus was shifted onto her all would have been well, but here she was sipping on a peach Bellini ice tea and wishing she had left when she had a chance. "So Gwen, what's up, you have been in your own world lately?" Next thing Gwen knew, she was pouring out her heart as Linda handed her a napkin to wipe away her wall of tears. "Ok now, let me see if I understand -- you have found this terrific man saved, sanctified, filled with the Holy Ghost and your problem is what? Sounds like a winner to me!" Linda said with laughter. "Gwen, you deserve to be happy. Why can't you just let yourself relax and enjoy what God is doing?" Gwen shrugged her shoulders, not bothering to answer. Linda didn't understand! She knew Linda had a past life before church, but hers didn't seem to chase her down or stalk her, like hers did no matter how hard she ran she couldn't escape it…. in fact, to be honest, Linda didn't even look like she had ever been on crack; there was no residue of anything but church on Linda. It was as if her past had never existed. Gwen knew she probably wasn't being realistic, but she longed for the day when all people would see is the new her. The woman that was beautiful and confident… the "Her" that had been reinvented and believed anything was possible. Right now it seemed as if that day would never come. She felt as if she had been sentenced to death row and she was sitting inside her cell listening to the footsteps as the guards approached, the sound of the clicking of their shoes down the long hallway, the shallowness of her breath ringing out the torture of knowing each breath brought her closer to death.

She was waiting for the jingling of the keys as they unlocked the bars, not to her freedom but to her demise, and that is what her past was for her: death by lethal injection. How could she tell Linda that it was not Max that posed the problem; the problem was her! She begin to feel a little juvenile; here she was carrying on, and she wasn't even sure how he felt, she wasn't even sure how she felt. One thing she was sure of was that she was bad news! Why had she let herself say those three dreaded words, "I wonder if?" You know the words that let your mind wander into uncharted territory. The words that let you sit alone and see yourself happy and picture what kind of life you would have. The words that let you create a custom-made life in which you could be anybody or anything you wanted to be. The words that let you dream. Gwen had never allowed herself to think about the "what if's" because it left you vulnerable. And she couldn't bear to be vulnerable; the what if clause had one flaw in her life: it required her allowing another person in! Was she ready to let Max in? She felt that familiar void begin to invade her heart, and she quickly excused herself. She had every intention to go to the restroom, but almost as if her feet had an alternative plan, she found herself racing past the bathroom and into the parking lot and to her car. She could barely see through her tears, she felt her heart pounding and her hands felt like pins and needles poking through her veins. She needed to get far away....What was she really doing? She had to put a stop to this; she knew deep down inside things would never be able to work out with Max. She just needed space, a chance to think!!!! She hit the curb, crushing a plant in her haste to leaving the parking lot. She glanced in her rearview mirror and heard that familiar voice, "Gwen you can run, but you can't hide," it taunted! She sped up and looked at the small letters printed on her mirror "warning: objects are closer then they appear!" She sighed, isn't that the truth!

Max sat reasoning with himself, why couldn't he just have fallen in love with someone who was not so complicated? It would have made everything so much easier if he could have made his heart fall for Erica, who was Deacon Howard's daughter. He was one of the founding members of his grandfather's church. All would have been good as far as his grandfather was concerned. She was "First Lady" material; she was beautiful and chaste, a lovely girl from a prominent member of society.

Yeah, they had gone out for coffee a few times, but as far as he was concerned, it had gone totally south when she had suggested that they take their relationship to the next "level". She had promised it would be their little secret. He had left her sitting right there in the coffee shop with his untouched espresso. She had tried to talk to him several times since that day, each time just to be greeted with a cold stare and a no thank you! He had hoped she would get the clue and leave him alone, but he had to admit this woman was relentless. She had told him the Lord told her that it was okay to sleep with her ....because she was his wife. Well, God definitely hadn't spoken anything like that to him, and in fact he was mortified, to say the least, when she had come by the church weeks later while he was working late one Saturday. She entered into his office wearing nothing but a choir robe!

"Surely even a man of your stature has needs, doesn't he?" she said. "After all, I know it's been a long time for you," she said, as she sat on his desk, resting one foot on the chair where he sat. He couldn't say he wasn't tempted; she was beautiful, but the thought of sharing himself with someone who had shared herself with ever man of the cloth within a 500-mile radius was not at all appealing. He was repulsed that she paraded around the church like a sheep in wolves clothing. She was not the virtuous woman his grandfather had thought she was. Needless to say, he had only one need -- that was for her to stay far away from him!

He sighed heavily one more time. The fact still remained: no matter how many times he reminded himself that he was going to take things slow, he seemed to be falling faster. Yes, it seemed like she was all he could think about, no matter how he tried. Here he was sitting at a meeting with the board members of the church. He was supposed to be helping them do what? He couldn't even remember anything but her beautiful smile, her soul-searching eyes, and her childlike disposition that she tried to cover up with her sassy woman mentality. Max knew that deep down inside there was an awesome woman of God. He had never had a woman that had been able to penetrate that spot that he had long ago closed off and declared out of order. He had given really no thought to family, thinking that, like the Apostle Paul, he was destined to be alone and a bondservant to the gospel. But right before him when he blinked, he could see a two-story house where he sat on the veranda watching his children as they ran giggling, engaged in a game of hide-n-seek. His children would never suffer the heartache that had plagued their parents' childhood or feel the torment of their innocence being stolen away from them. He would sit there and smile as He stared into their daughter's eyes as she wrapped her little arms lovingly around his neck. Her eyes were so full of life; he would hoist her high above his head, complaining that she was way too heavy to reach the stars. He would bring her down suddenly to a shower of kisses. She would throw her head back, sighing in contentment because she knew she was safe in his arms. And he was determined that his little princess would know that her daddy loved her very much.

Next to their house was a stable that housed the horses they rode up a trail leading to a place he had built just for them. It was a place away from the hustle and bustle of life. They had spent many nights erasing all the years of pain they had suffered … This was a special place where he would lift her in his arms as he had done many times before and carry her over the threshold, pausing to kiss her. As she laughed, she would tell him he was a hopeless romantic, but deep down inside he knew she enjoyed every doting moment, and into the little cabin they would go. He would gently sit her on the couch as he lit the fireplace. The crackle of the flame would engulf the room; he loved to sit and talk to her sharing every aspect of her thoughts…. He would brush the grey streaked hair off her forehead as he would thank God that they had shared fifty years together, and he would pray that God would grant them fifty more because he knew no amount of time would ever be enough with Gwen! He knew with her he could never grow old. He would forever see the little girl that had captivated his heart what seemed like a lifetime ago.

Deacon Howard cleared his throat, jarring him back to reality. "So, what's your answer? You are the last to vote. Max could feel the bead of perspiration begin to roll down his forehead. Suddenly it got hot in the room. He felt a little faint as he nervously took a sip of the room- temperature water. Uh, could you repeat the question please? Max didn't know what he was supposed to answer. He tried very hard to concentrate, but his mind continued to trail, taking on a journey of its own. They all snickered and exchanged seemingly mystified looks although they punched each other indicating that they were not as clueless as they pretended to be. "So who is she?" asked Elder Clement. Max wondered how the church people always seemed to know when something was going on. "Look at that, Claiborne! He got that 'deer in headlights' look!" laughed the old man. "Ain't nothing but a woman makes you to look like that, he snickered. "Yes, I reckon you right, Cleo. You is a pro when it comes to that sort of stuff, ain't you!" laughed Claiborne. Yes, Rosa-Lee Claiborne was a beautiful woman was and quite witty. Most men were intimidated by her wit although she was small in stature but huge in mouth. Cleo, hmm…. she was the only one who dared call him by his first name; after all, he was an Elder. "You will always be plain old Cleo to me! She spat one day when he had attempted to correct her when she called him by his name in front of the board. That woman drove him insane, but for some reason he could never really get her out of his mind or out of his heart for that matter. Now these two…now here was a strange relationship. They never seemed to be interested in each other but at the same time of not "being interested", last summer Rosa-lee Claiborne had announced her undying love the day Elder Clement was due to wed Brenda, a mild-mannered schoolteacher. She immediately took it back after she had ruined their wedding day. It was kinda sad, the two of them -- too much pride to ever admit that they needed each other. So, here they were continuing their cat-and-mouse game.

You going to just sit there or are you gonna answer?" Elder Clement asked intently. "Umm, what was the question?" asked Max, sheepishly. His grandfather shot him a disapproving glance. His gaze softened some after he became aware that Elaina was scowling right back at him. Elaina was the one who had been there to help him when his dear Helen had lost her long fight with breast cancer. He had once been filled with life, and now he was just a stubborn old man. Long gone was the passionate side of him; she had a way of tapping into Sidney's human side. They had spent almost all of their life together. She was the one who would swoop in and fix his messes. She was the voice of the people of the church … That side had left fifteen years ago on Christmas day when she had slipped out of his life forever. She had been his one and only, and the old goat stayed stuck in his ways. Elaina had heard about Max's little romance with Gwen, and she also knew that Sidney wouldn't hear of it. He was dead bent against it. He was an old fool who had been trapped into bitterness by his broken heart. Erica is the best choice -- he had reasoned. That blind bat couldn't see anything if it was right up on him. Erica was a floozy. Hmm…she always tried to put her best foot forward in front of her, but she could see straight through that demon. "I'm worried about pastor, Elaina. He seems lonely," she had said to her. She didn't even have the decency to pretend like she had any respect at all. The nerve of this girl to call a seventy-year-old woman by her first name! Yeah, that girl had the devil in her eyes, parading around the church like she was so concerned about him. This girl was no angel. Max was a good man, and he deserved to have someone who had passion. Now, Gwen had issues, wasn't no use in lying about it, but that girl was special. She was everything that Max needed, and Elaina was gonna have to get Sidney to see that, somehow…

She looked at him, sitting there glaring at poor Max. He had forgotten what it was like to be a young man in love! Why did he have to be so pigheaded about everything? She supposed everything would have been definitely different had Helen still been alive. After all, she was the "reason" behind the man. And Elaina felt her heart aching… here she was wasting her time on someone who would probably never be able to love her. She would always be in the shadow of his dear Helen. She had been in love with him for over ten years, but the big brute, no matter how much she loved him; she had to admit he may never let her in. Well, he can stop his own chance for happiness, but one thing was for sure, she was not going to let him ruin her Max's chance! He was the closest thing she had to a son, and she was certain of one thing -- he was not gonna turn out like his grandpa, trapped in the church with no life and afraid to take a chance on love!

You gonna just sit there, or are you gonna answer?" asked Mother Holmes again. "Umm, what was the question?" asked Max sheepishly. His grandfather shot him a disapproving glance. "Just continue with the plans. Let's just reconvene at another time when Max is able to function," Sydney said. Max tried to look busy fiddling with files, trying to avert the accusing looks and smirks as the board members tipped out one by one. And he was left alone with his grandfather, who sat quiet for what seemed like an eternity, whose eyes were piercing into the very soul, leaving nothing left to expose.

"Care to tell me what the deal is? And don't say 'nothing' because now it is affecting your decision-making process and that affects my church!" Sidney was an attractive man. He was a man who seemed gentle upon first glance, but he was a man of wisdom whose stature commanded respect. Max had always understood that when it came to church, he was serious. That's why he was so surprised to find out that he was chosen to succeed his grandfather after his health had begun to fail. Lately, Sidney had given almost all the decision-making process to him.

"Max, listen, I have heard a little news that seemed quite disturbing. Are you seeing a woman named Gwen? One of the members of the church seemed to have seen you leaving her house in the early part of the morning." Max knew eventually he was gonna need to talk to his grandfather, but resentment began to rise up in him. He had done nothing wrong, and he did not like where this conversation was headed. He listened as his grandfather made it clear that this was unseemly behavior for a pastor. "Flee from all appearances of evil, son." The bible says that we are to live above reproach. He had taken more than his fill when his grandfather attempted to inform him of Gwen's little escapades. He found himself standing and staring square in his grandfather's eyes, something he had never done, and said, "Well, this unseemly woman is gonna be my wife. And not you or any of these nosey church folks know her. I love her; I always have and if that means giving up my seat, so be it"… and turned around, allowing the door to shut on his way out, jetting past the board members scampering out of the hallway pretending not to have overheard the argument. His heart was beating so fast; his eyes were blurred as he stumbled toward his car fumbling for his keys and praying he would have enough strength to drive as he closed the door and strapped the seat belt firmly around him…although this safety device did nothing for his life -- that seemed to be headed for a head-on collision.

~

After driving around for what seemed like forever, Gwen pulled up in the driveway leading into Robin's house. She hadn't talked to her in so long; why was she here? The truth was that she missed her friend. Robin was a piece of work, but right now she felt like she just needed something familiar. "You don't need to be here! Danger…Danger… Danger!" sounded the alarm in her head. "I'm just going to see how she is doing. I am not doing anything wrong," she said as she brushed off the little sirens wailing in her heart! Everything in her was telling her to go back to the car and drive away, but she sighed as she knocked on the door. The door opened, revealing the most beautiful woman she had ever seen. Wow, she must have been at least six feet tall. She had fiery red hair and blue-grey eyes and flawless almond toned skin. Her posture was strong and commanding.

"You gonna stand there staring at me or are you gonna say something, shorty?" the woman said. "Yes umm, is Robin here?" Gwen stammered. The woman rolled her eyes, obviously annoyed.

"Yeah, she here," she said as she stepped back and swung open the door. "Come on in, you might as well make yourself comfortable," the woman said. As she led her into the living room where Robin was sitting on the couch, Robin looked up, smiled and tapped the spot right next to her, indicating a place for Gwen to be seated.

Gwen decided to take a seat on the sectional facing the couch instead, which apparently amused the two women. They laughed like someone had just told a funny joke. As quickly as she had appeared, the beautiful woman disappeared somewhere as a phone rang in the other room.

Wow, Gwen, didn't think I would be seeing you anytime soon.... What brings you here?" she said as she rummaged through a carton of cigarettes, retrieving the last one and carelessly tossing the package on the coffee table as she lit it with shaky hands. "Hey, Monica, bring me a drink." An awkward silence followed. Gwen shifted in her seat; she was repulsed by each breath of the second hand smoke she inhaled. She could not believe that the woman who sat before her had ever been her best friend, and now she stared at a complete stranger. Wow, it seemed like such a lifetime ago that they had once shared everything, and now they appeared to have nothing in common.

After what seemed like an endless amount of time, the beautiful woman came in with a dry martini; with a smile she leaned down and planted a seductive kiss on Robin, who immediately tensed up. "What's the matter, baby, you don't think your little friend is going to be embarrassed do you?" she said coyly. "Monica, knock it off." Gwen could see that Robin was a little flustered. "Well, there is enough to go around," said the woman brazenly with a laugh. "Ok, Monica, that is enough," Robin said, obviously embarrassed. "Monica go and get our guest a drink; oh, I forgot, you can't drink can you?" she said as she snickered, obviously back to her old self. "How about a coke, you can have soda or is that against the Ten Commandments, too? Thou shall have no caffeine." Robin was a barrel full of laughs today. She laughed long and hard over her own joke. "Yes, a soda would be good, just not a Coke. How about a Sprite?" Gwen said as she slumped back on the sectional. "Look, it's Coke, Ms. Prissy, we don't have any Sprite," said Monica sarcastically. Robin interrupted, "So, why don't you go to the store and get some and while you are there, get me cigarettes." Monica was obviously disturbed but seemed to have decided going to the store wouldn't be so bad. She took one more look, her blue-grey eyes lingering a little too long for Gwen's taste, making her uncomfortable. "It's too bad, shorty, we could have had fun." She winked and blew her a kiss. "You are kinda cute," she said and laughed as she left the room.

It was Robin who broke the awkward silence. "So, why are you here? I haven't talked to you since you started riding your high horse into your land of make believe, pretending you like them church folks." In truth, Gwen didn't really know what she was doing here. She felt so out of place.

Robin waited a little while for her to answer and then threw her head back laughing. "You are a real straight arrow now, aren't you?" Robin said in disgust. "Well…. I remember when you weren't." She laughed coyly. "You come in here looking like you are a real church girl," she said, as she looked her up and down as if inspecting for one sign of the old remnants of what once was. Finding none, she decided to take a trip down memory lane.

Gwen paused a minute; she hadn't told anyone about this part of her life. In all actuality, she was hoping it would all just fade away, leaving no trails of existence. It wasn't like she and Robin had ever been in a relationship. They had messed around a few times, but in their group who hadn't? It was a part of that lifestyle - - you know, part of the fantasy she had fulfilled for those men whose wives wouldn't. The night she had left Brian frustrated and confused about his rejection she had run to Robin for support. One thing had led to another, and she found herself intertwined into something she was hoping she could forget. "Umm hmm, I remember when we used to know each other very well," Robin glanced consciously, and Gwen dropped her gaze.

"What if your church folks knew about that? You think they would look at you the same?" she jeered. "No, we are the same sweetie, you and I, we are made for the streets; we know what we want and who we are gonna use to get it," she said as her eyes sparkled, amused. Suddenly her gaze softened, "Yes, we are alike; have you forgotten -- it's always just been you and me." She said, "We've had some really good times, don't you remember? Isn't that why you are here? You missed me? Robin got up to sit next to her, a little too close for her comfort. "Our life wasn't that bad, was it?" she said, reaching out to gently stroke her hair. "I heard you been dating a little preacher man. You really think he'd still love you, knowing our little secret? He doesn't know you like I know you. If he knew about me, what would your little man of the cloth say? Ha ha ha, she chuckled. You are keeping it on the down low, baby, hmm. I like the secret lovers thing…makes me feel kinda 007," she laughed. "You are good at hiding stuff, aren't you? Does he know about our little extracurricular activities? Gwen, don't you want me like I want you? Ever since the last time, that's all I have been thinking about - how it felt to hold you, to kiss you." Robin leaned even closer and began to kiss her neck. The sweet smell of her perfume heightened her senses; her breathing deepened.

She was flooded with old memories, almost as if a door had been opened, revealing some of her most private moments. She swallowed a deep breath of air, suddenly realizing the room was stuffy. Her heart began to beat faster. She wanted to run through the door and take hammer and nail and shut it, never to remember any of this again. But her body stayed wedged to the couch. "Come on, feet don't fail me now,"

She prayed, but despite her plea, defiantly neither her legs nor her feet put forth any effort to move. And to her dismay, her body began to come alive almost as if it needed to be held. It had been so long since she had seen that look in somebody's eyes. Robin

wanted her; she desired just to be caressed. She was confused --
why was her body betraying her? Her breathing began to
accelerate. She reasoned with herself, "I can stop anytime; just a
few more minutes." She closed her eyes, giving in to the ripples of
passion that traveled through her body as Robin's hands began to
explore and awaken parts in her that she had forgotten herself.
Gwen felt like she could not control herself; the passion began to
swell deep within her. It was like fire started in her toes and raced
up her spine and into her head, stopping and making her head
woozy before it started the process all over again.

"Don't you remember; we were good together? You were
always so beautiful, Gwen, but you have always been off chasing
after people who didn't love you. Honey, you can change your
clothes and attend all the bible studies you want to but inside of
you will always be a void. I have always loved you," she said, as
she wrapped her arms around her trying to pull her closer. Gwen
closed her eyes, trying not to remember, but how could she not?
"Robin, I am not proud of the things I have done in my life, but I
really have changed. I met Jesus, and I am not the same," she said,
desperately trying to convince either herself or Robin - she wasn't
sure. But she was sure the shakiness in her voice wasn't too
convincing.

"You were off on those escapades when all along I have been
right here. See, I know you. I have always known you. I accept you
for who you are. I know your little boyfriend doesn't know you
like I know you. Do you think you are ever gonna be good enough
for those church folks? Don't you remember how they would
watch us, those crazy men knowing they could never please you
like I could?" Her voice sounded thick as it was littered with
lustful desire. She pushed her back on the couch as she began to
push her body close to hers, sending electrical currents racing
through Gwen's body. Gwen knew this was a battle she was
quickly losing. "Just give me a little time, honey, I will help you
remember," she said as she began to unbutton Gwen's blouse.

"Mmm hmm, it won't take me long"….It felt like her body was gonna explode; she just wanted to let go and just enjoy how good it felt to feel another body close to her. She panted. "Oh, my God," Gwen thought, "what am I doing? I shouldn't be here!" Her eyes flew open, and she was met by the scariest thing she had ever seen. It had three heads - one like a bull, one like a man and the last like a ram – and the tail of a serpent, which switched to and fro. It laughed as she struggled to get up. "Who are you?" she stuttered. This beast straddled her …there was nowhere to go! "What do you want….Who are you?" she screamed. "Asmodai," he replied. "Don't you remember me? I have visited you quite often." Out of its mouth was a forked tongue that pointed, accusing in her face. It had the most repugnant smell she had ever smelled; it was like bad eggs and burning flesh. "What do you want?" she exclaimed, trapped under the weight of this hideous beast. "What do you mean?" it said. "You want me!" "Oh God," yelled Gwen. "What have I done?"

Kathleen sat eating chocolate ice cream and Fritos, welcoming each spoonful as she looked though tentative sketches for the cover of her book. She had kept herself busy writing and now all that was left was to submit her work to Erica, her editor. This was much different from her normal work; she felt vulnerable and exposed. She had poured out her heart and soul and now her very essence would be held in someone's hands as they read. She wondered if the stories would do justice to the lives that they portrayed. Well, one thing was certain: in a few short weeks she would be a mother. She thought back on all that had transpired between now and then, and it seemed like a lifetime ago. Now her baby would soon make her debut, and for the first time, she was excited! "It's you and me, Paige", she said, "and one crazy auntie Shirley!"

Nicole sat on the couch, trying to find something to watch when she heard the doorbell ring. Everything in her told her not to open the door. She saw Spencer. She had not seen him since that day he flipped the script and told her he didn't want her or the baby. She opened the door and could immediately tell that he had been drinking as he pushed past her, making himself comfortable and surveying the whole room. "So, you thought you would just start all over, take my baby and do what? Live the life of luxury?" he said. "Spencer, you need to leave. I don't have time for this!" she said, as she shut the door and tried to contemplate her next move. "Well, make time for me. You living in your fancy house and working your stupid job. Now, you too good for me, huh? Ain't nobody gonna ever want you but me," he said. Her rebuttal was fierce: "No, I didn't have time for you when you threw me out and tried to make me abort my baby!"

He stepped back like he was stunned but quickly recovered. "I'm just saying...how do I know the baby is mine? I didn't come to fight with you; I came to see you. I've missed you baby…you don't miss me…come on, no one loves you like I love you," he said, as he softened his gaze and stumbled toward her, leaning in real close to her face.

"Come on baby; make me happy," he said, blowing his hot beer breath on her face. "Spencer, you need to leave!" she said, as she tussled to free herself from him leaping up, but he was fast. He grabbed her, pulling her close to him as he plopped down on the sectional. "Leave me alone!" she said, struggling to get free of his grasp. He was too strong; she felt a small pain beginning in the bottom of her back. "Girl, I've missed you," he said, as he held her forcefully against him.

"Spencer, I need help!" she pleaded. "What you want me to do? I don't know nothing about no baby," he smirked. "You alright, do some of them breathing things in and out," he said jokingly. "You need to leave me alone!" she said.

"I'm not going nowhere until I get what I came here for!" he said."You belong to me. Don't tell me what you ain't gon' do; you gon' do what I tell you to do," throwing her with so much force she hit her head against the wall.

Chamber seven

Gwen let the shower wash over her body, trying to get rid of that creature. How she got away from that thing and home, she didn't know…Her tears couldn't be distinguished from the flow of water that trickled from the showerhead. He was fearfully paralyzing. She shuddered as she thought about him. She looked over her shoulder just in time to see the black cloud scurry away. She knew somehow deep in her heart, she hadn't seen the last of Asmodai.

"I don't hate you, Shirley. I never have. I just have never known what to do with you." Shirley's mom was barely audible, but the words rang loudly in her ears. She struggled to shut them out; she stared at her mom who looked so little and frail. For the first time in her life, it looked like her mother had a sense of compassion in her eyes. "I'm sorry." The words Shirley had waited her whole life to hear suddenly did nothing but infuriate her. How could she stand there, looking at her like she wanted her to do what with her sorry? To forgive her and let her die in peace when her whole life had been a nightmare!

"You don't understand, Shirley. I didn't know how to love you. You reminded me of what he did to me. Every time I see you, I see him. You don't think I know I've never been a mother to you? You don't think your daddy reminded me of every flaw I had concerning you? It wasn't hard for him, but he wasn't the one that was violated. He wasn't the one that had to carry that bastard's baby…..her voice trailed off. Shirley could see she was fatigued. In her mind, echoing over and over again were the words, "bastard's baby".

Shirley stood looking out the window, wondering how her mom must have felt. She had never thought about how her mom was a victim just like she was in all of this. How do you raise a child that reminded you of the worst day in your life, reliving it over and over? Why did everything have to be so difficult? Her whole life, she just wanted to be someone; she wanted to be seen, heard, and loved. Daddy had been the only one who had made her feel like she wasn't a mistake, something that just happened. "Mama, why did you wait so long?" Shirley heard the little girl in her trying to get out. "Why have we wasted so much time fighting?" she said, as the tears began to cascade down her face.

"Ah, my spirited one, everything is as it should be," she said, as she reached her arms for Shirley to come to her. Shirley allowed herself to fall into her mother's arms as she sobbed on her shoulder. She felt her mom pull her closer, and she closed her eyes and tried to forget all the times her mom's arms never comforted her, the times when her sweet embrace eluded hers. "Why, God, why?" she said. She wanted her mother's arms to hold her for the rest of her life. She wanted her mother to be proud of who she had become. Just then, Shirley heard a loud crash downstairs. She left her mom's embrace reluctantly and walked out the door, but all the preparation couldn't prepare her for what she saw as she entered her living room. Nicole was lying seemingly lifeless with a big gash on the side of her head and a pool of blood was gushing from between her legs. She hurriedly dialed 911. Next thing she knew, she was surrounded by flashing lights and everything was a blur, between police, ambulances and fire trucks. She prayed. "God, please save this baby," she said, as that familiar pain tried to creep its way into her scarred heart.

Shirley finished talking to the doctor. He assured her that all was well with Nicole and the baby. She had to have an emergency C-section when she arrived at the hospital. Shirley had tried to call Nicole's mother, but she had told her she wanted nothing to do with her.

She went to the gift shop and bought an "It's a girl" balloon arrangement. She peeked in the room and there was the most amazing sight ever: Nicole was holding in her arms a 7 lb 13 oz, 21 inch long miracle; she was beautiful. "Come in." Nicole motioned. "It's ok. I'm not trying to interrupt your moment."

Nicole looked at her, tears in her eyes: "She is beautiful baby."

"Thank you, had you not got there in time, I don't know what I would have done, Shirley!"

"What's her name, Nicole? She is perfect." Nicole looked at Shirley and said, ""See, that's what I was hoping you would help me with. I was thinking her mother could name her," handing the baby to her. "Her mother?"
Shirley repeated slowly. "I don't think I understand, Nicole, you are her mother."

"We both know I'm nobody's mother, but you are, and that's why I need you to be there for her and love her. Please! I've thought about this moment since I first met you. Shirley, you saved her life twice! I need you to promise me that you will teach her, so she won't make the same mistakes I've made in my life. Can you promise me that?" Nicole paused and waited on her to answer.

She shook her head, tears falling down her face. She remembered how she felt when the nurse had come and took her Destiny away. She held her new bundle of joy close and closed her eyes, inhaling the beautiful smell of her new baby, her new baby girl.

"What's her name?" Nicole asked. "I think we will call her Taielor Nicole," Shirley said, as she smiled through her tears.

Linda and Allen's wedding was beautiful. It was an honor to be a part of her special day. The "jazz under the stars" theme was a success. She surveyed the room, watching all the happy couples and wondering, "Would she ever have this? Today she had watched two people who were in love with each other enter into a moment where one plus one didn't equal two anymore, but it now became one.
Max slipped up behind her, pulling her close to him.

"You did an amazing job." He felt her immediately tense up, so he relaxed his hold. "Gwen, eventually we are gonna have to figure things out."

"What?" she said. Like how I will never fit into your fairytale life? How I am not "first-lady" material or had you not even noticed because you still see the little Gwen who needs you to save her, the little silly girl who was your project? He wasn't in love with her; he was entangled in her past; she was not that little girl anymore!

She wrestled away from his grip and swiftly walked away, heading out the door as quick as she could. She needed some air . She needed to get away from who he was trying to make her into. The fact remained that she was damaged and not even the great and powerful Max could fix her.

Linda made her way over to Max and could see the rejection in his eyes; she could tell he felt defeated

"Linda, I don't know what she wants from me. I love her. The truth is I've always loved her."

"Tell her," she said.

"My Gwen is a complicated creature; she is afraid."

"Afraid? Gwen isn't afraid of anything. She lives by her own rules and that dang woman won't let me get close to her!"

This girl made him so mad at times; she made him want to pull out his hair, one strand at a time and then, in the very next moment, pull her close and fix everything in her world. The truth is that she was like a wild horse that he would never tame but in reality, her freedom is what held him captive. None of that mattered now. Intertwined between their past (mining of the diamond), present and future. He pulled the ring from his pocket. At this time, the past, present and future met for one moment. Their past had been intertwined with pain but the present had been filled with endless hope and it was at this moment that he realized that he could not allow Gwen to slip from his grasp because a future without her was meaningless. He shut the ring box and was more determined than ever to get Gwen to understand that it wasn't perfection that he needed and that God had placed everything he needed in her. She just needed to know that she was his good thing.

Shirley hadn't known that she would never talk to her mom

again. When she returned from the hospital, her mom had slipped away in her sleep.

Her mother's funeral was small and intimate. She had hoped Camille would have come, but she made an excuse as she always did and, just like that, her life was changed.

She smiled as Brian came in with Taielor in tow; those two had been inseparable since she had brought her home from the hospital. She was six weeks old and just perfect.

She kissed him, grabbed Taielor and hurried out the door. She was excited to visit Kathleen and Paige, who had made her entrance into the world 2 weeks late. She was her mama's daughter, determined to do everything on her own terms.

Kathleen and Shirley sat looking at Paige sleeping peacefully in the crib. Danny would have been so proud of his little girl. She had started to wonder if Kathleen would ever truly be happy. She still wasn't ready to let go of Danny.

Shirley had tried unsuccessfully setting her up with Dr. Martin. They had seemed like perfect matches, but she hadn't seemed remotely interested.

Shirley's own love life had been great. The flame had been relit. She closed her eyes and remembered how it felt to be in Brian's arms again. Everything just seemed so right; in fact, they were secretly planning to renew their vows. She was just waiting for something to go wrong. Every time Shirley went to sleep, she was afraid she would wake up, and it would all just be a dream. Yes, life was good. Nicole's baby's father had gladly signed the adoption papers with the understanding that charges would not be pressed against him and that he would stay away from Nicole.

Her stomach started to bubble. She had been under so much stress lately, it seemed like her body would never get back to normal. She couldn't eat, she couldn't sleep, ugh, and her body ached all the time.

Kathleen was oblivious to Shirley's deep thoughts as she was happily chatting away about the upcoming party. It was sort of a "welcome home Taileor" party, which is why she didn't understand why the party had to be formal or why she had to invite Gwen. But, she agreed only because she hadn't had the energy to fight with her. After all, it was her party. Just then her phone rang, startling her. She stepped out the room so as not to awaken the baby.

"Hello," said the familiar voice." I know you said you would call me, but I just wanted to hear your voice. Did you tell Shirley yet?" "No, I'm just waiting on the perfect time to tell her," she whispered. "I mean, everything has been crazy. Vincent, let me do this in my own time, ok?"

"That's Dr. Martin to you!" he said laughing. She glanced nervously in the room at Shirley who was still clutching Taielor and cooing at Paige, who had awakened from her short catnap. Why she was taking so long to tell Shirley that she and Vincent were together, she didn't know. Why was she being so childish? Maybe it was because admitting that she liked Vincent meant moving on from Danny.

"Kathleen, Brian invited me to the party and I don't want Shirley to find out and think we have been hiding like some little kids." "Vincent, ok. I will tell her!" "Tell me what?" said the voice behind her. It was Shirley. She hurriedly hung up the phone. "Who was that?" she asked, "And why are you acting so strange? What's wrong? Is something wrong with you? Oh my God, is something wrong with Paige?" She fired so many questions, Kathleen couldn't answer until she finally blurted out, "I'm dating someone…that's it!"

Shirley looked at her stunned. "I thought we said no more secrets. Heifer, come on with the come on, who is he?"

"His name is Vincent." she said softly. "You know him as Dr. Martin."

Shirley screamed so loud, she startled the baby. Taielor began to wail, and Paige started as if on cue. Kathleen didn't mind, though, it was a welcomed interruption. She wasn't ready to face reality, not yet.

Gwen sat in her car, wanting to drive far away, but where was she going to go? She was tired of running.

Max opened the door and slid in next to her. "Max, I don't want to talk," she said. "Well, that's good 'cause what I have to say does not require you to say anything. I love you and have loved you from the moment I met you. I have faulted myself for not protecting you, but I am here now, and I'm not leaving. You are not my project, but if you would have me, I want to make you my wife. I want to spend forever with you, not wasting one moment. Let me hold your hand until you can give me your heart." She stopped crying and looked at him, searching for his eyes to tell her he wasn't serious, but she was met by a look of determination. This was all too much. She stumbled out of the car. It seemed like everything slowed down and there he was – Asmodai, standing over her. "He doesn't love you," he spewed.

"You are wrong," she said, "I'm not afraid of you anymore. I'm not running anymore. She understood now. In order to be the woman she was created to be, she had to let the little girl go. Asmodai took one-step forward, and she yelled loudly, "Get thee behind me, Satan," and he disappeared. Max stood in front of her: "I'm not letting you go," he said as he dropped to one knee. "Marry me, Gwen! It's always been and will always be you, girl." She looked at him and the crowd who had begun to gather around, no one daring to breathe, and she heard herself whisper, "Yes…yes….yes" she said louder each time. He leaped up and pulled her to him as the crowd cheered.

Brian smiled as he saw Shirley come into the room, glowing. She wasn't even dressed yet. She was wearing a plush robe but he couldn't take his eyes off her; she was getting Taielor dressed. She was a good mom, and he had to admit he was quite surprised when she had come home excitedly and told him that Nicole wanted them to adopt her baby. But all of his fears had been washed away the moment he looked into Taielor's beautiful brown eyes. She was the most beautiful baby he had ever seen. Her hand reached up and touched his cheek, and he knew he would forever do whatever it took to make this little girl happy. Today they had invited a few friends to their surprise renewing of their vows; it was difficult to keep it a secret from all of their friends and family, but today was finally the day. He took Taielor so he could give Shirley the last few minutes to get ready to join the party. Shirley went into the bathroom and splashed water on her face.

Today was the day. No one knew, not even Kathleen, why they were here, but today was a new beginning, a day that they would celebrate their life together. She opened her purse and shakily pulled out a pregnancy test. She was wondering if she was stressed, or maybe it was something more. Her period was more than 6 weeks late. She was a mommy of a 12-week old baby, and she was probably wrong, but now was as good as time as any to check. It was hard to pee on a stick. She took the test and stood waiting to see what the results would be. "Shirley, what are you doing? Open up," Kathleen said, as she pounded on the door. She unlocked the door to see her friend, beautiful in her gold dress. "Hi," Shirley said. "You thought I wouldn't find out," she said, clutching a beautiful rose bouquet. But stopped talking as soon as she saw the pregnancy test lying on the counter.

～

Gwen and Max were the first guests to arrive, and Brian smiled as he saw them together. She finally had what she wanted, a man who loved her. Taielor was the star of the show. She kept the guests busy as they arrived one by one. Everyone gathered outside and soon realized tonight was much more than just a formal dinner party when they were ushered outside to the beautifully decorated backyard. Brian stood next to Vincent. He was surprised that they had gotten so close so fast, and he was excited to find out that he and Kathleen had been seeing each other. As he stood waiting for Shirley to join him, he remembered the last year: He had almost taken his life, lost his wife, and given up on everything. Now, he had a beautiful daughter, and all was well.

"You ready?" Kathleen said, as she zipped Shirley's dress. They had agreed to wait and look at the results until after the wedding, which was killing Kathleen. They walked into the hallway and Kathleen remembered she had left the bouquet. She ran back in to grab it .Then they made their way through the house and out where everyone was waiting for the beautiful Shirley. Shirley paused one moment and just for a second wished her daddy was there to walk her down the aisle.

Kathleen couldn't help but smile as Brian and Shirley pledged their love to one another again.
There was not one dry eye at the wedding. It was over as quickly as it started, and everyone was seated and eating. Kathleen figured this was as good a time as any, so she stood up to give the toast. "Shirley and Brian, we have been through so much together, but I want you to know that there are not two people more deserving than you two. Congratulations! And one more thing before I sit down: Taielor is gonna be big sister soon," she said. "You know, I had to peek." The whole room exploded in excitement.

Shirley pretended to be mad, but it was short lived when she saw the joy that filled Brian as he grabbed her, dancing her around the room.

Kathleen stared down at her ring finger. She realized tonight – in order to be happy, she had to let go of the past. She took a deep breath and pulled it off and slipped it into her clutch. Where was her life headed? She didn't know, but one thing she was certain of -- she couldn't be happy and live in the grave.

"Goodbye my love," she said. As she saw Vincent motion to take her hand and lead her to the dance floor. She smiled at Shirley as she laid her head gently on his shoulder. She closed her eyes and for the first time, she felt safe and knew she was destined to live. She was fully persuaded to ride this out and see where it led her.

About the Author

Tears in the Chambers of Heaven

Trinisha Marks is a native of Las Vegas Nevada , where she resides with her high school sweetheart and husband of sixteen years Kevin Marks. She has six children ranging in ages from 17 to 10, who she would fondly describe as rambunctious.

Trinisha is an Elder of New Beginnings Ministries where she serves as Pastor Smiths secretary. She is a graduate from Cheyenne High School class of 96 , has a Bachelor's degree in Psychology and is working on her Masters in Marriage and Family Therapy.

Trinisha has many hobbies but is passionate about her writing which includes plays for community theater and church productions. Baking is one of Trinisha's favorite things to do a few of her signature dishes include her peach cobbler, seven up cakes and organic muffins. Her motto Is, "If you can think it I can bake it." Her future aspirations is to see her work come to life on the big screen.